A Jedi uses the
Force for knowledge!

THE PHANTOM BULLY

by *New York Times* bestselling author
Jeffrey Brown

Scholastic Inc.

Thanks to everyone who helped make this series a great experience to create, and a better story to read: Joanne, Frank, Leland, Carol, JW Rinzler, and everyone else at Lucasfilm; Marc, Chris, Brett, Steve, Phoebe, and all my other editors, publishers, and colleagues; my friends and family, especially Jennifer, Oscar, and Simon; all the readers who've been so supportive and responsive; and everyone at Scholastic who got this book out into the world in the best shape possible. Finally, extra special thanks to Rex Ogle, for being an editor when he needed to be, a friend when I needed him to be, and quite often both at once.

www.starwars.com

Scholastic Children's Books
An imprint of Scholastic Ltd
Euston House, 24 Eversholt Street
London, NW1 1DB, UK
Registered office: Westfield Road, Southam, Warwickshire, CV47 0RA

First published in the US by Scholastic Inc, 2015
First published in the UK by Scholastic Ltd, 2015

ISBN 978 1407 14501 3

A CIP catalogue record for this work is available from the British Library.

Printed and bound by CPI Group (UK) Ltd, Croydon, CRO 4YY
Papers used by Scholastic Children's Books are made from wood grown in sustainable forests

7 9 10 8

www.scholastic.co.uk

A long time ago in a galaxy far, far away. . . .

There was a boy named Roan Novachez (that's me), who was FINALLY becoming a REAL pilot at JEDI ACADEMY! Now he's starting his final year there, and it's probably going to be REALLY, REALLY hard, but it's also going to be really AWESOME!

Me at the end of last year
Me at the start of this year!

Hey, Roan, we heard you have a girlfriend at Jedi Academy.
Well, sort of. I don't know if she's MY GIRLFRIEND exactly...
But at least you finally got to fly in a real starfighter.
Well, a real star pilot simulator.
Oh. A simulator.
Hmm.
I've been driving a real SoroSuub Corporation repulsor Combine harvester.
Really? Those have pretty difficult controls, right?
Yeah, it takes a while to get the hang of...
That's cool, Adam!
I can lift things with my mind.

Hey, Ro.
Roan, are you Jedi now?
Not yet.
I'm be a Jedi.
Watch.
ROAN! I DID IT!
Good job, Ollie.
Mom, I did it!
Did you check the mail yet? I'm waiting for a couple letters...
Mail? No one uses mail anymore.
Mom! I did it! I used Force!

Hi, Mom. When is the mail coming? Gaiana sent a letter, and I'm waiting for this year's welcome packet from Jedi Academy.
I thought the mail came already.
No, it hasn't yet.
Yes, it did. Didn't Dav give you your letters?
Hunh?
Oh, this one?
From Gaiana?
Hey!
What? I didn't open it!
How is Gaiana's dad doing?
A lot better.
This came, too. From Jedi Academy.
Are you ready for your last year of middle school?
Yeah, I messed up last year, but I'm going to be super-focused this time.
Roan, I can help you if you not ready.
Thanks, Ollie!

WELCOME BACK AGAIN TO JEDI ACADEMY

As students return for their final year at Jedi Academy on the planet Coruscant, their Padawan training will enter a new and exciting phase. Each Padawan will be paired with a Jedi mentor for individual instruction. They will also choose a specialized area of focus, such as healing, piloting, or farming. Padawans will finish the year well-prepared to continue on their path to become Jedi.

This year, Padawans will focus on their unique abilities in a number of ways, including the class talent show. Students will have the chance to show off their favorite hobbies and hidden skills. The individual strengths of each student will also be measured in the Padawan Obstacle Challenge Trial, where teams of students must work together to solve problems and get through barriers using their strongest skills. In order to finish their training at Jedi Academy, Padawans must also complete the Jedi Labyrinth Trial by finding their way through a maze while defeating other students in lightsaber duels.

PENTADAY

This summer break was a lot shorter than last year. At least, it seems that way. It helps that Gaiana and I have been talking and writing to each other all summer. Pasha also came to stay with me for a few days. I thought he was going to be really bored, but he said Tatooine is so different from where he grew up, it was really fun for him. I leave for school next week already, and this time I think I finally really know for sure what I'm doing. Plus, I'm not going to get cocky like last year, especially since I have to work with Mr. G. for my one-on-one training. As long as I can make it through, it's okay if it's not perfect. Unless Mr. G. ends up making me as grumpy as he always is...

Bye!
Roan, aren't you forgetting something?

I remembered underwear this time. Journal, comic supplies, books...
No, I think I got everything.

Oh!

We love you!
Love you, too.

Actually, I think I DID forget my underwear?!

STUDENT: ROAN NOVACHEZ

LEVEL: PADAWAN | SEMESTER: FIVE

HOMEROOM: MASTER YODA

CLASS SCHEDULE

0730 - 0850: HABITS OF USING THE FORCE
Master Yoda will help students make the Force a part of their everyday routines.

0900 - 0950: PRACTICAL MATH
Mrs. Pilton will show students how to apply math skills to useful tasks, such as buying things.

1000 - 1050: CREATIVE WRITING
Under the guidance of Librarian Lackbar, students will develop expressive new writing.

1100 - 1150: ETHICS OF JEDI MIND TRICKS
Principal Mar will teach students principles to consider before attempting mind tricks.

1200 - 1300: LUNCH BREAK

1300 - 1350: INDEPENDENT STUDY I
Students will spend intense periods working closely with their assigned Jedi mentor.

1400 - 1450: LIGHTSABER ACROBATICS
Mr. Garfield will team up with Kitmum to teach students more dynamic moves for lightsaber duels.

1500 - 1550: ADVANCED STAR PILOT TRAINING
Mr. Garfield will train students using star pilot simulators of increasing difficulty.

Pasha!
Roan!
Here, let me carry your suitcase!
Oh! Let me get yours for you!
You guys realize that makes no sense, right?
Hey, Bill.
Hey, Bill.
BOOP BWEEEEP!
Oh, sorry, RW-22! Hi!
pat
pat
pat
I think he missed you!
BEEP BLOOP!
Or he wants us to carry him around using the Force, instead of our suitcases?
BWEEEP?!
Don't worry, I'm sure he was joking!
BEEP BO BLEET!

Roan!
Gaiana!
BONK!
Giggle!
Giggle!
Giggle!
Oops.
Oof!
Ouch!
BUMP!
What?
Go giggle somewhere else.
Some of us are trying to get through here.
Don't let him get to you.
I won't. Are you okay?
Yeah.
CAUSING PROBLEMS, MR. NOVACHEZ?
What?! No!

GOOD. IT'S GOING TO BE HARD ENOUGH TO TRAIN YOU, WITHOUT YOUR USUAL MISBEHAVING.
Must... not... respond!
Ugh. I can't believe he's going to be my Jedi mentor all year.
Who's your Jedi mentor, Gaiana?
Librarian Lackbar.
Mine's Principal Mar.
I've got some new Jedi...
I have M'Ba-Tee, the Jedi who visited last year.
I wonder who's training with Master Yoda?
Guess.
What?! No way!
Heh heh! Good to work with you, it will be, Cyrus.
You guys would tell me if Jedi Academy was conspiring against me, right?
Of course!
Sure!
Unless we were in on it...
Yeah.
Just kidding!

The Padawan Observer

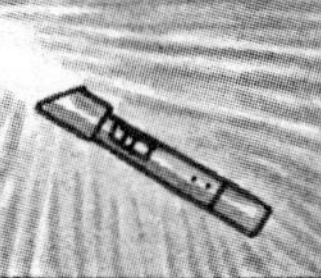

EDITED BY THE STUDENTS OF JEDI ACADEMY · Vol. MXIV #1

WELCOME BACK ALREADY!

Another year at Jedi Academy has begun after what some students describe as a long summer break. "It seems like FOREVER since I've seen my friends!" exclaimed an excited Shi-Fara. Teachers, however, had a different view. "Hmph," Mr. Garfield stated. "Why even send these kids home every summer if they're going to come back so soon?" Padawans enjoyed an all-school picnic where

they met their independent study Jedi mentors, many who are former teachers and students from the Coruscant Campus. Gammy says there is leftover Potato Slug Salad if anyone would like more to take home.

INSIDE:

TRIDAY

I was going to try and stay positive in this journal entry because I'm happy to be back at Jedi Academy and seeing Gaiana and Pasha, but AUGGGGGGHHHHHHH, MR. G.! All of us spent time meeting with our individual Jedi mentors and already Mr. G. is making it impossible for me.

I thought Master Yoda was supposed to be the wise mystic with confusing sayings! The two classes after my independent study are with Mr. G., too. It's going to be a long school year. It won't be so bad, since I have good friends to relax with. We decided we're going to have a board game night once a week. Gaiana and I were on the same team and won the first game, which is totally the perfect start to the semester!

Before class, introduce a new student, I must.
Transferring from Ossus, Lilly is. Show her today's exercise, can someone?
Hi.
Basically, you need to use the Force to make a sandwich. It's really hard and takes a while to get it right, so try not to screw it up too much.
Okay... like this?
Whoa!
She's awesome!
Nice!
Whatever. She didn't even use the ham.

HEPTADAY

Yesterday, we met a new transfer student in class. I remember when I was the "new kid." It was rough! The new girl, Lilly, is REALLY good using the Force, though. She even beat Cyrus in lightsaber fencing class. Even Mr. G. was impressed, and of course it was a perfect ~~oppartunity~~ opportunity for him to point out how much training I still need. Lilly felt bad about Mr. G. comparing me to her, and said she was just trying to do her best, but we told her not to worry. That's how Mr. G. always is. Gaiana invited Lilly to sit with us at lunch. We found out she's vegetarian and doesn't eat any meat. The strange thing about that is she was vegetarian BEFORE she even tried Gammy's cooking!

Ha! I guess you shouldn't have been going easy on her.
I wasn't!

Hey! Why doesn't your pasta have eye-meatballs?
Maybe we should be vegetarian.

holobook ▸ Discussion ▸ What's your focus?

Each Padawan will focus on their own specific area of study this year. What are you studying?
POSTED BY L. LACKBAR

I'm going to study music.

I'm studying dance, we should work together! Er, individually as a team?

I'm focusing on interactions between the Force and nature.

I think you'll be a natural at that!

"Natural?" I get it, ha! Let me guess your focus... star pilot?

I figured everyone probably knew that already!

I didn't. I thought you'd focus on being a klutz.

Why don't YOU focus on being positive instead of negative, Cronah?

Yeah, aren't you still on academic probation? You should be nicer.

Lightsaber fencing.

That was my choice, too! Is that allowed?

Hee hee!

Mrs. Pilton, Roan and Gaiana are passing notes. It's very distracting.

Let me see the notes you're taking, Roan.

You missed one of the equations, Roan. Make sure you double-check these.
Wait, not THOSE notes...

One of these days, Roan...
phew!

DUODAY

I've been having a lot of fun with Gaiana in class, because we're study partners, but Cronah is trying to ruin it. He even got Ronald to start making fun of me. Ever since I came to Jedi Academy, Cronah and his friends have been out to get me. I would say it's because HE likes Gaiana, but I don't think Cronah likes ANYONE. Last year, I probably would've gotten advice from Yoda (about dealing with Cronah, not about Gaiana). I can't talk to Yoda about anything lately, because he's spending a lot of time as Cyrus's individual instructor. I can't talk to Mr. G., that's for sure! That's why Pasha's such a great friend—we can talk about anything. He's been dating Shi-Fara a while, so he has lots of good advice. Like, I should just ignore Cronah... I think I already knew that, too!

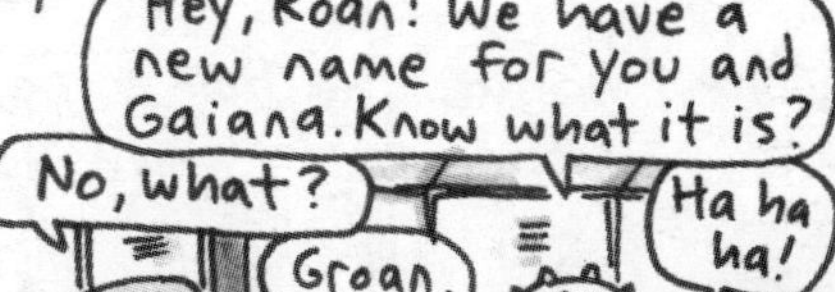

Hey, Roan! We have a new name for you and Gaiana. Know what it is?
No, what?
Groan.
Ha ha ha!

Uh, Mr. G., can I talk to you about something personal?
NO. HMPH.

MIND TRICKS

Notes

A Jedi can use the Force to influence the behavior of others

- When using the Force for mind tricks, make sure you wave your hand properly.

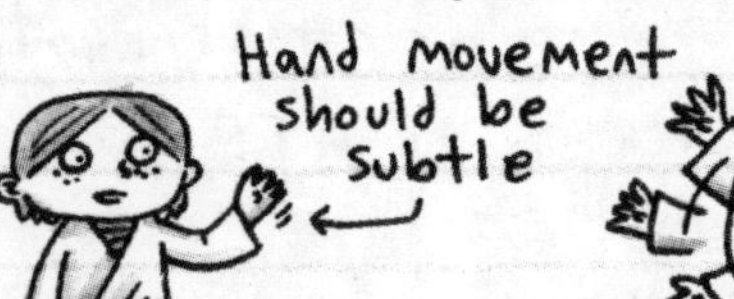

Hand movement should be subtle

Too much!

- Mind tricks should never be used for profit or gain.
- Using mind tricks on your friends will lead to you not having any friends to use mind tricks on.
- Begin by practicing mind tricks on your pets.

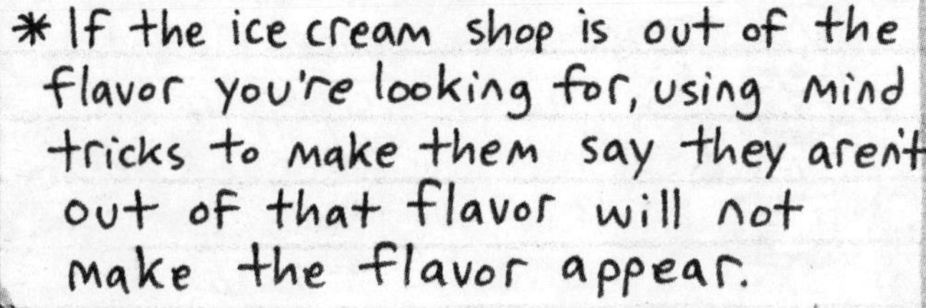

Sit!
I said, sit!
C'mon, sit!

* If the ice cream shop is out of the flavor you're looking for, using mind tricks to make them say they aren't out of that flavor will not make the flavor appear.

Oops!
TRIP!
Roan, look out!
SPECTACULAR CATCH!
You're out, Cyrus!
You, too, Cronah!
Bonk!
Sorry, Bill!
BONK!
Nice try, Tegan, but you're out!
Bonk
That's it for you, Mary!
Bonk!
That was fun!
Can we play again?
Didn't she say she never played dodgeball before?

Things Yoda communicated to us this week
A Jedi is not reckless.
Think carefully about his words, he does.
But not for too long, or look weird, he will!
A Jedi's communication skills flow from his mouth.
To be understood, speak clearly, he must.
Quicker, easier, mumbling is... but confusing!
Train yourself to make eye contact, you should.
Hmm. Forgot to blink, I have.

holomail

FROM: master_yoda_642
TO: Padawan Class Group
SUBJECT: Important Field Trip Information

OPTIONS
◁ REPLY
▷ FORWARD
□ PRINT
○ POST TO HOLOBOOK

WHEN: WEEK THREE
WHERE: THE PLANET NABOO
PURPOSE: To study environmental impact by various societies on different habitats, and learn conservation strategies using the Force.
ACTIVITIES: Students will observe wildlife in its natural habitat and captivity, swim in Lake Paonga, and visit the Gungan Sacred Place.
NOTES: Students should plan on taking notes for post-field trip essay writing. Students should not worry about sando aqua monsters, which hardly ever get near the student swimming area.
CHAPERONES: Yoda, Librarian Lackbar, Kitmum, and RW-22.
ITEMS TO BRING: Swimsuit, sunscreen, swim goggles, waterproof notebook, binoculars, scuba gear, towel.*

*Make sure towel is not waterproof or it will not dry you off.

You can see how these grass plains are still affected by the nearby city of Theed, while areas like Lake Country are nearly untouched.
I better take some notes...

A good student takes lots of notes.

But make eye contact and nod head so she knows I'm listening.
Mm-hm.

Repeat information to remember it better.
So Lake Country is only accessible by speeder.

Remember to ask questions.
How do they make sure people don't build on the plains?

Roan, you look tired... is this too much walking?
No... paying attention is exhausting!

MONODAY

Naboo is Gaiana's favorite planet to visit, so the field trip has been fun. Yesterday we visited the Gungan Sacred Place. It didn't look sacred to us, because it was all ruins grown over with plants in a swamp. Master Yoda explained that respect for nature is maybe part of what makes it sacred, although not even our Gungan guide knew <u>why</u> the place was sacred. It still looked really cool! Tomorrow, we're going swimming in Lake Paonga. I'm kind of nervous, because I've only ever swam in a swimming pool before.

Roan, we're all going to jump off the diving rock, want to come?
Uh...sure?
That looks deep!
Ha ha!
Wheee!
splash!
Scared of sando aqua Monsters, Roan? I don't blame you!
They probably go after the weakest first. Ha!
C'mon in, Roan!
I guess I shouldn't worry...
Okay, here I- OOPS!
SPLASH!
Roan! Are you okay?
Why d-didn't anyone t-tell me how c-cold the w-water is?

HEXADAY

Train yourself to let go of everything you fear getting wet.

Leave your dry clothes and shoes on the shore, you should!

Master Yoda decided we should do team-building exercises at the lake, so we had swimming relay races. My team wasn't doing well, because I'm not a great swimmer. Unless I'm compared to other kids on Tatooine, since there's no water there! My team didn't get mad at me, though, they just started coming up with funny swim styles, which was way better. I started feeling like the "new kid" again, until we went to the shaaks farm. Our Gungan guide showed us how to ride the shaaks, and it isn't that different from riding dewbacks on Tatooine. I even gave Lilly some tips until she got the hang of it. Then she started doing tricks! Everyone was impressed. Again. She's totally the coolest kid at our school now.

She's kind of a show-off.
Yeah. I like her.
Guys! Try this!

Before we went to the Naboo Zoo, Gaiana seemed really quiet. After what happened last year, I decided I should just talk to her. At least then I'd know if she was mad at me. It turned out she was actually feeling insecure, because Lilly is good at everything and everyone likes her. So it made Gaiana feel weird when I was helping Lilly out with riding the shaaks. I told Gaiana I was just trying to be more helpful now, like Pasha was with Gaiana's dad last year.

She said I was sweet. She even tried to kiss me! On the cheek. But I turned my head by accident, so she ended up kissing my hair instead. She laughed, so it was okay. At the zoo, she showed me around. When we saw the voorpaks, the zookeepers asked if we wanted to care for one at Jedi Academy again. Voorpee is coming back with us! I'm going to make sure nothing happens to him this time.

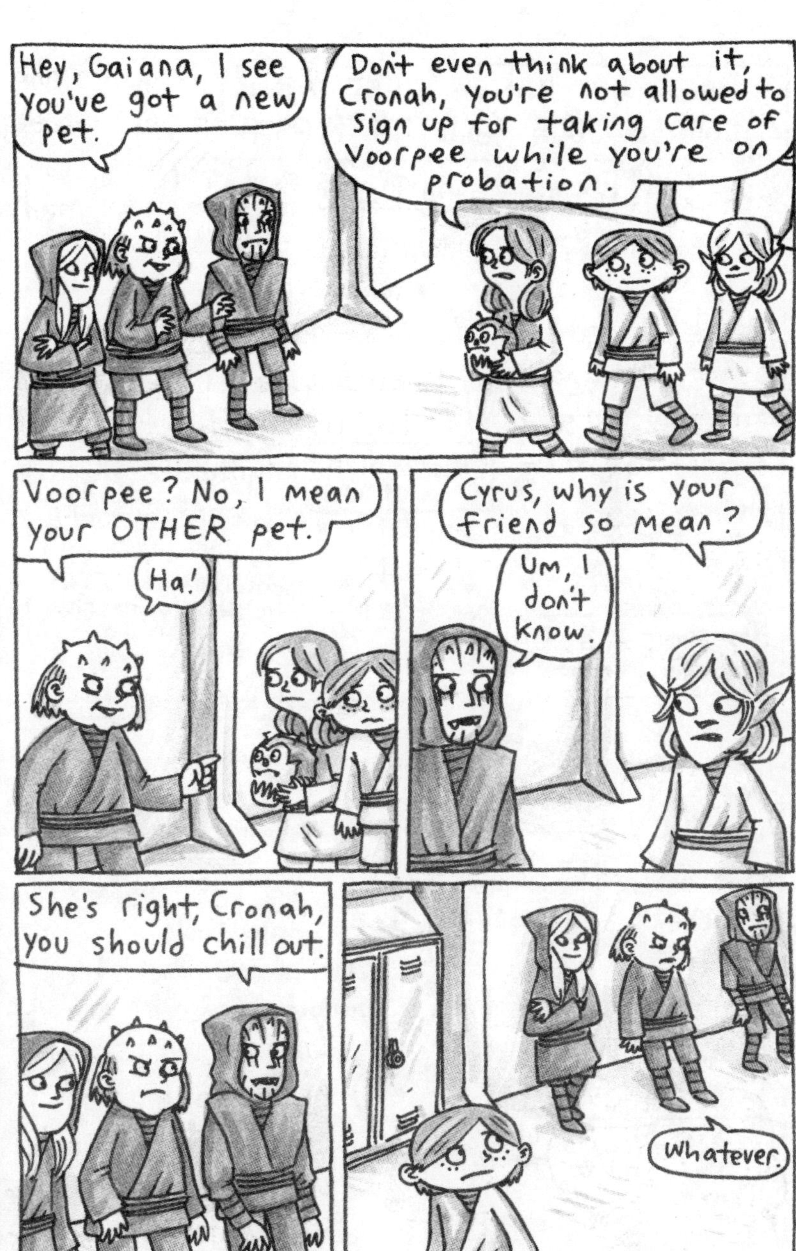
Hey, Gaiana, I see you've got a new pet.
Don't even think about it, Cronah, You're not allowed to sign up for taking care of Voorpee while you're on probation.
Voorpee? No, I mean your OTHER pet.
Ha!
Cyrus, why is your friend so mean?
Um, I don't know.
She's right, Cronah, you should chill out.
Whatever.

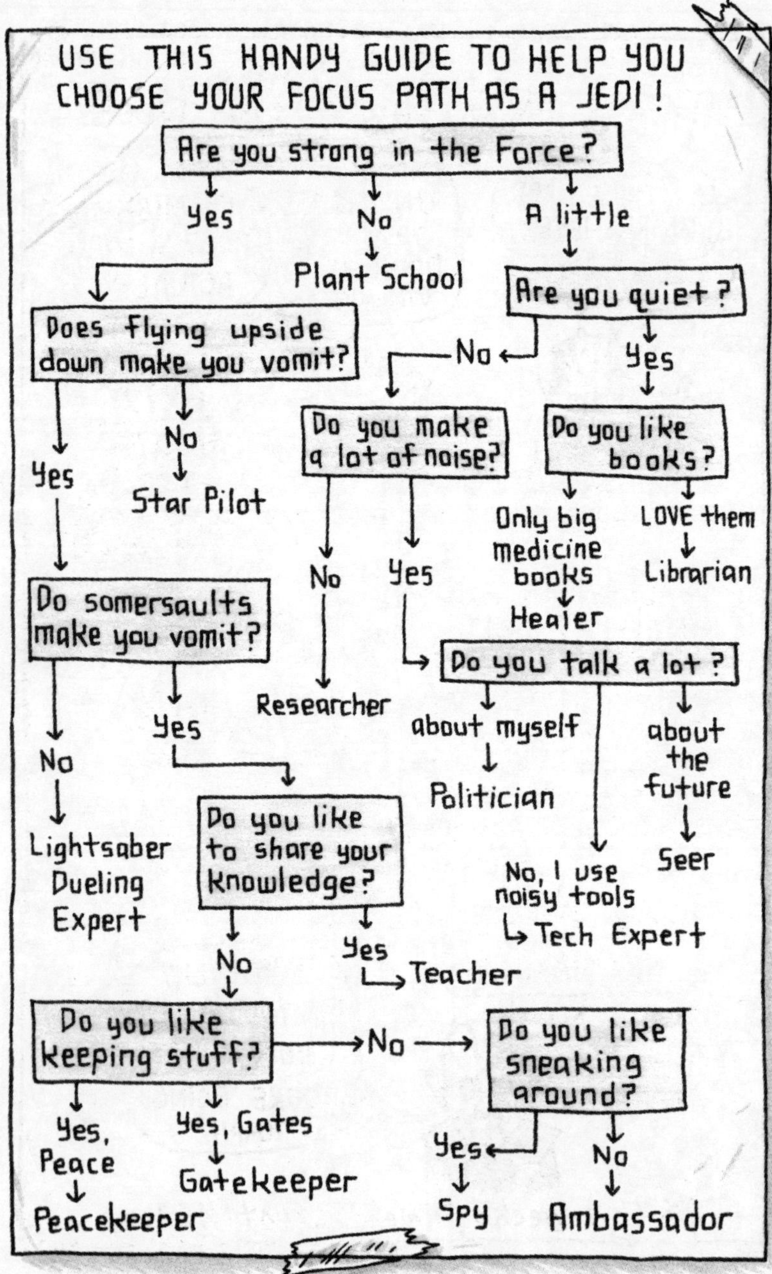
USE THIS HANDY GUIDE TO HELP YOU CHOOSE YOUR FOCUS PATH AS A JEDI!
Are you strong in the Force?
Yes
No
Plant School
A little
Are you quiet?
Does flying upside down make you vomit?
Yes
No
Star Pilot
No
Yes
Do you make a lot of noise?
Do you like books?
Only big medicine books
Healer
LOVE them
Librarian
No
Researcher
Yes
Do somersaults make you vomit?
No
Lightsaber Dueling Expert
Yes
Do you talk a lot?
about myself
Politician
about the future
Seer
No, I use noisy tools
Tech Expert
Do you like to share your knowledge?
Yes
Teacher
No
Do you like keeping stuff?
Yes, Peace
Peacekeeper
Yes, Gates
Gatekeeper
No
Do you like sneaking around?
Yes
Spy
No
Ambassador

Things Mr. G. said to me this week

A LITTLE HARD WORK NEVER HURTS.

HMPH. UNLESS YOU'RE DOING IT WRONG.

IT MIGHT HURT A LOT, ACTUALLY.

ALL WORK AND NO PLAY WILL ACTUALLY MAKE YOU THE BEST AT WHAT YOU DO.
SO NO PLAYING.
EVER.

WORK SMARTER, NOT HARDER.
ESPECIALLY IF YOU DON'T KNOW WHAT YOU'RE DOING. HMPH.

* This week's "Hmph" count: 453

straighten
Fidget
Ready for our double date, Roan?
No, but if we don't go now I'm going to be all sweaty!
Wait! What are those?!
Flowers.
Oh, no! I didn't get any...
Don't worry, I got you covered!
Phew, thanks!
Hey, Gaiana!
Hey, Shi-Fara!
Hey, guys!
I hope it's okay if someone else comes along?
BWEET?
Oh, my! I wasn't planning on it, but RW-22 and I would be honored to accompany you!
BLOOP!
Oh, er, T-P30, we meant...
This will be delightful, I am so happy!
BEEP BOOP TWEET!

Actually, Lilly was wondering if she could come with us?
Sure!
Who's your date?
Hey, guys.
Hey... Cyrus.
Hi.
Thanks for letting us come with.
Oh, sure.
what's he up to?
Hey, Roan, can I have one of your flowers?
Uh...
Thanks!
Hungry for some pizza?
Yeah.
Relax...
Oh, thanks!
Ah, pizza! Did you know that traditional Nabooian pizza toppings include...
Hee hee!
...but on the other hand, proteinleaf is popular with...
...I read that, it's good!
Have you seen...
Mm-hm!
Anyone want another slice of cheese?

Oh, no! I forgot my wallet!
It's okay, I'll cover you, Roan.
Oh, thanks...
I'm so full!
We don't have to be back to our dorms for an hour. What should we do?
If I may suggest, the soccer field bleachers offer a splendid view of the sunset.
But we need a teacher to go there after school hours.
I suppose if I take you, that would be allowed, as long as we leave right after.
Did you guys know Lilly's team won the Adega System Soccer Championship?
Really?
Our team almost made regionals once!

QUADDAY

My first official date with Gaiana last night was awesome! I didn't spill anything on myself or Gaiana, I didn't say anything embarrassing, and I didn't accidentally ruin it. Gaiana is funny and cute and smart. She's also the nicest person I've ever met. The weird part of our date was that Cyrus came along with Lilly. And he was super nice! Maybe now that he's working with Master Yoda, Cyrus does want to focus on being a Jedi instead of being a jerk. Or he's just behaving because he's on probation. He seemed nice last year, and ended up totally trying to ruin my year. So I need to be careful, because I wouldn't be surprised if this was part of some plan he has with Cronah. Cronah seems in an even worse mood than usual lately — if that's even possible. This morning he totally tried to trip me, and most of the time he's just saying stuff. Maybe Cronah will start pretending to be nice like Cyrus.

Roan, what do you think of the new star pilot simulator software? Any tips?

Oops! Sorry, Roan.
Hey!

HAVE YOU CHECKED YOUR LIGHTSABER CRYSTAL?

Prevent accidents! Remember to change your crystal once a year!

PADAWANS IN THE NEWS

- Jedi Academy student Pasha contributed to a research paper by his father, published in the new issue of Jedi Archaeology.
- Transfer student Lilly was honored with a plaque and restaurant gift certificate for her contributions last year to the Jedi Academy Ossus Campus debate team.
- A profile of Student Council president Ronald Rinzler was featured in the Coruscant Senate Bulletin.

Ewok Pilot

By Roan Novachez

HOLOSEARCH

You searched for....'Roan Novachez'
0 results found.
REFINE YOUR SEARCH.

Did you mean....'Ronto'?
31,100 results found (.35 Galactic standard seconds)

RONTO
Strong but docile beasts of burden, Rontos are commonly used by the Jawas of Tatooine for...

RONTO FOR SALE
Elderly Ronto for sale. Still works hard but is really, really slow...

RONTO CENTRAL
Your source for your Ronto supplies...

Images for...'Ronto'

Hello, class. I'm Gub Vendo, your substitute teacher today while Master Yoda meets with the, uh, Galactic Senate.
So, er, yes, well, let's see, um, I'm sorry, give me... a moment...
Can't seem to find...
Lesson plan...
Excuse me, Mr. Vendo?
Yes, er — you?
Cronah.
Yes, Cronah?
Would you like me to help?
Oh, thank you, yes!
Maybe I should teach the class for you?
That will be such a help to —
uh.
Excuse me?
You obviously don't know what you're doing, right?
Ha ha!
Um... I don't know?

TRIDAY

I felt really bad about what Cronah did to our substitute teacher, Mr. Vendo, yesterday. Not just because it was mean, but because I didn't say anything. At first, nobody said anything, but then Gaiana and Lilly did. Gaiana is always good like that. I wish I could learn to stand up for other people like she does, but even when I think of saying something, I don't, and by the time I'm ready to speak up, it's too late. Like, weeks late. I did tell Gaiana it was good of her right away. One thing she and I have been doing together is taking care of Voorpee. The little voorpak has really warmed up to me, even after last year's drama. I'm sure his liking me has nothing to do with the extra treats I've been feeding to him.

Can we NOT have Cronah teach? I want to actually learn today.
You don't have to be such a jerk, Cronah, geez.

He really likes you! It's like he wants to live in your pocket...
Yeah, heh heh!

Roan, we're heading over to the Archives to study, want to come?
Yeah! Mr. G. gave me a bunch of homework I need to finish.
Just let me grab my backpack.
Oh, I thought I put it here...
Oh. Maybe I left it... no?
I know I had it here, didn't I?
Maybe I left it in my room?
Uh, I'll catch up with you guys...
Ok.
It's not here. Where could it be?
Watcha doin', Roanie? Writing love poems?
IGNORE IGNORE IGNORE IGNORE IGNORE IGNORE IGNORE IGNORE IGNORE

HEXADAY

Someone took my backpack and I KNOW it was CRONAH! If hate wasn't the path to the dark side, I would say I hate him, but instead I'll say I really, really, really, really, don't like Cronah. I would've thought it was him anyway, since he keeps saying stuff that totally shows he's in on the prank. Pasha agrees that it was probably Cronah, but he, Bill, and Egon all told me not to worry, and they'll help me look for it. Gaiana and Shi-Fara even offered to let me use one of their bags until I find mine. Having friends rules. At least my journal wasn't in my backpack—that would've been a DISASTER. Especially if Cronah was reading it. It's still kind of a disaster, because all of my star pilot training notes and workbook were in it. I'm going to have to work extra hard to make up all of that work. I know Mr. G. will have ZERO sympathy for me.

Roan, did you just get BACK from somewhere?
Huh?
It felt like you were MISSING.
Class seemed less PACKed than usual.

Today, cook with Gammy, we will. Use the Force to make meals, you will learn.
Hurgh!
URN MRGHH ERF!
Did you understand what Gammy told us to make?
No...
...but with Gammy's taste in food, does it even matter?
Good point.
This isn't too hard.
Can you pass the salt?
Sure.
Time to taste these.
How did so much lemon get in mine?!
Eep!
You look pretty sour about how yours turned out, Roan.
He looks like Yoda.

I know Cronah took my backpack!

Hmmm... he wouldn't really still have the same locker combination after last year, would he?
Aha!
CLICK!

Smells like old socks! Let's see... ew, sticky...
I don't see it...

MR. NOVACHEZ! WHAT ARE YOU DOING? IS THAT YOUR LOCKER?
Uh-oh!

Uh, no, it's Cronah's, I think he took my backpack and—
YOU NEED TO LEARN TO BE RESPONSIBLE FOR YOUR THINGS, ROAN.

AND YOU NEED TO LEARN TO NOT MESS WITH OTHER PEOPLE'S BELONGINGS. I THINK DETENTION IS IN ORDER HERE.
But—
HMPH.

DUODAY

Well, my backpack was found. Fortunately, everything was still in it! UNfortunately, whoever took it filled it with leftover food and put it under a table in the cafeteria. For a minute, I got excited, because I realized there's a Force ability where you can sense the history of an object, and Silva's focusing on being a detective for his individual training. He couldn't sense who took it, though, because the backpack was too messy. I feel stupid for not redoing all my star pilot training homework already. I was doing it kind of slowly because I was hoping it would be inside whenever I found my backpack. I'm still sure Cronah did it, but maybe he had help...

Let's see... I sense... moldy grainmush... it was in a bowl. And there's some pickled zog... half eaten.

Ew, gross!

The Usual Suspects

ROAN, I THINK I KNOW YOUR PUNISHMENT FOR GOING INTO OTHER STUDENTS' LOCKERS.
I thought detention was my punishment!
And it was only one locker!
HMPH. COME WITH ME.
Where are we going?
YOU'RE GOING TO LEARN HOW TO TAKE CARE OF SOMETHING – BY WORKING ON A REAL JEDI STARFIGHTER!
Is this one of those lessons where I learn by getting what I actually wanted?
What?
Are we going to fly now?
HMPH. YOU MISSED A SPOT HERE.

PENTADAY

It's hard enough getting all of my own work done without having other people asking me to do work for them. I don't know why Ronald tries to get ME to do all his work for him. He's focusing on politics with his Kaminoan Jedi mentor, and asked me to illustrate the essay he's writing. I told him I didn't have time, and Ronald acted annoyed and grumbled about me drawing stuff for Gaiana. First, Gaiana has never cheated off me. Plus, she helped me with math class. And . . . I like her. I don't know why Ronald's Jedi mentor would let him use other people's work. Kaminoans are supposed to be experts at cloning, maybe Ronald should clone himself and he could get twice as much work done.

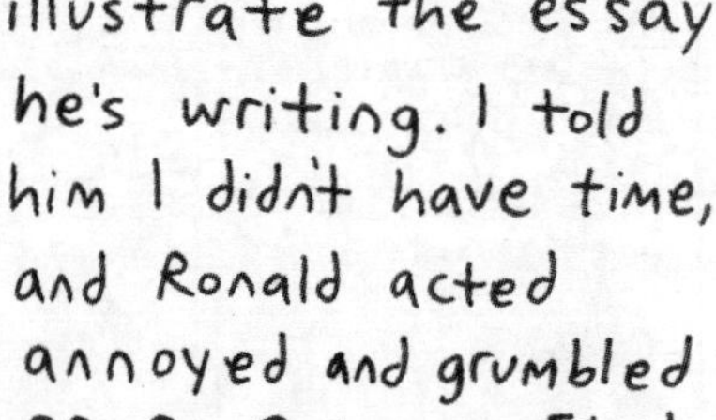

Or he would just cheat off twice as many people. I wouldn't mind having a clone. That way, Mr. G. could be mean to the clone instead of being mean to me . . .

JEDI MENTOR SPOTLIGHT #3

With each Padawan studying under an individual mentor, Jedi Academy has a number of new guest Jedi teachers. In this issue, we continue our series introducing readers to two more of our visiting professors.

NORI HA is a Kaminoan Jedi whose expertise in biology and genetics is unmatched in the Jedi Order. Nori also writes the popular manners advice column "Jediquette."

Teaching for the first time, GUB VENDO is an Aqualish Jedi Knight, best known for his lightsaber dueling techniques to use while injured. Clumsy as a child, Vendo dedicated his life to perfecting graceful movement.

Ewok Pilot

By Roan Novachez

Hey!

AAAUUGGHH!

Augghh!
Ahng!
Ohhhh!

Cronah, she didn't even touch you.
Yeah.
Urgh!

Penalty kick!
Ronald, you realize you're not a referee, don't you?
Penalty kick, sweet!

I thought you were injured!
I'm a fast healer.

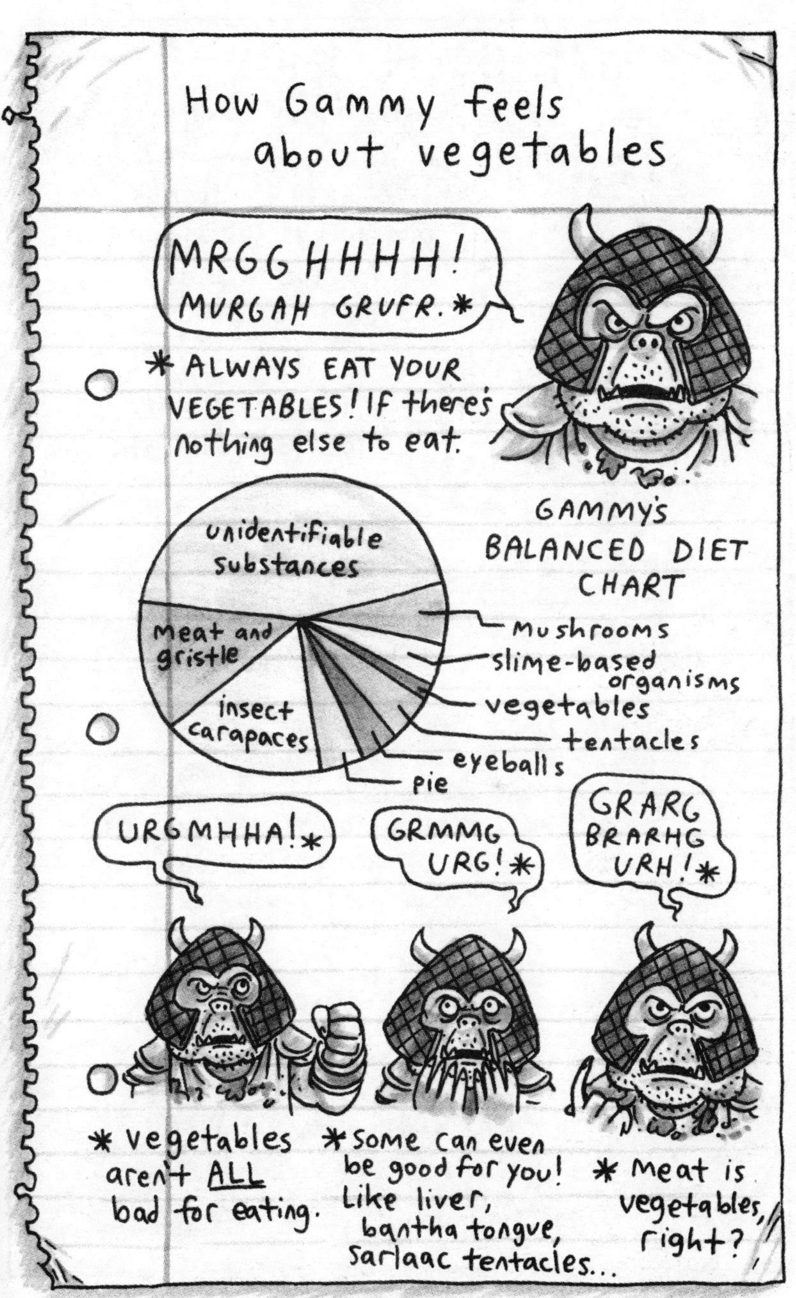
How Gammy feels about vegetables
MRGGHHHH! MURGAH GRUFR.*
* ALWAYS EAT YOUR VEGETABLES! If there's nothing else to eat.
GAMMY'S BALANCED DIET CHART
unidentifiable substances
meat and gristle
insect carapaces
mushrooms
slime-based organisms
vegetables
tentacles
eyeballs
pie
URGMHHA!*
GRMMG URG!*
GRARG BRARHG URH!*
* vegetables aren't ALL bad for eating.
* Some can even be good for you! Like liver, bantha tongue, Sarlaac tentacles...
* Meat is vegetables, right?

Stuff Guest Jedi Mentors said this week
Face new challenges- practice with one arm tied behind your back.
Easy for Master M'Ba-Tee to say!
Use the Force!
But use the bathroom first if you need to.
We are all unique... that is why it would be great to clone ourselves. We would be twice as unique!
The Force will be with you, always.
Remember that before you pick your nose.

Roan, do you want to draw a comic with me?

Yes ☒ ← Hey, there's only a "yes" box and it's already checked?

Yep! You start!

Today's debate is Ronald and Lilly in favor of settlement by the Trade Federation on the moon of Endor, while Roan and Bill advocate for leaving the Ewoks alone.

As you know from our colleague Roan's comics, Ewoks are a *primitive* species that could benefit from new technology.

The benefit would clearly all be to the Trade Federation, not the Ewoks, who would be exploited along with their natural resources.

Funny you should talk about exploiting Ewoks, Roan, considering how much you profit from drawing them.
My mini-comics cost more to print than I sell them for!

Er, actually, I think the bigger picture is that in order to make the Endor moon a better place for the Ewoks, there will naturally need to be some benefit for the Trade Federation.

"Natural" is exactly the word I'd like us to remember here. The Ewok's culture would be destroyed, along with their ecosystems.

Speaking of Ewok culture, Bill, I notice, as a D.J., you steal a lot of Ewok beats.

It's called remixing!

What does Bill's music have to do with Endor?

Both of you just use Ewoks.

The fact is that the Trade Federation will empower Ewok society, and lead it into a new Golden Age!
clap
clap
clap
clap
clap
clap
clap
clap

I think the standing ovation shows I'm the clear winner here, Roan.
It's only one person.
Still, he's standing.

clap
clap
clap
clap
clap

HEXADAY

The class somehow voted that Ronald's team won (by <u>ONE</u> vote) in our debate, even though what he was saying is OBVIOUSLY wrong. It didn't even feel like a debate, since mostly it was Ronald ~~interrupting~~ interrupting us to say something kind of personal. And talking about stuff that didn't have anything to do with Ewoks or the Trade Federation. Bill and I ended up spending our time responding to Ronald instead of making our points. We could have done better. Lilly wasn't happy, either, though. She apologized to us for what Ronald was saying, and for not speaking up more. It really bugged her that she didn't get to say more, and win the debate by actually... debating?

Roan, didn't you lie about the Voorpaks? Are you lying now?
Roan, how can we trust your facts, with your history of exploding science projects?
How can you claim to speak for the Ewoks? Are you, in fact, an Ewok?
Ugh, so annoying.
I'm so annoyed.
That was soooo annoying.

Poor Roan... still haven't gotten a new backpack?
No time. Still catching up on homework.

Well, we got you a new one!
It's neon green!
With a baby Ewok attachment!
Because you like Ewoks!

Oh, yeah...it's... great. Uh, thanks, guys.
Kind of small, too...

Don't you like it?
Uh, no, I love it! It's great!
Heh.

Just kidding, Roan! Here's the backpack we really got for you!
You guys are cruel. But also the best!
We thought you could give the other one to Ollie.

holomail

FROM: MR_GARFIELD_THE_6TH
TO: PADAWAN CLASS GROUP
SUBJECT: OSSUS VISITING STUDENTS!

OPTIONS
◁ REPLY
▷ FORWARD
□ PRINT
○ POST TO HOLOBOOK

ATTENTION, ALL CORUSCANT JEDI ACADEMY STUDENTS!

THIS WEEK, STUDENTS FROM THE OSSUS JEDI ACADEMY OFF-CAMPUS EXPLORER PROGRAM WILL VISIT OUR SCHOOL! SINCE LILLY KNOWS THEM, SHE WILL ACT AS THEIR GUIDE, BUT DURING THIS VISIT, ALL STUDENTS ARE EXPECTED TO ACCOMMODATE OUR GUESTS!

YOU WILL BE REPRESENTING OUR SCHOOL, SO PLEASE DON'T MAKE ME FIND NEW WAYS TO MOTIVATE YOU TO BEHAVE WITH RESPECT, OR YOUR FAILURE WILL BE COMPLETE!

AND I DON'T WANT TO HEAR ANY COMPLAINING! HMPH!

Hey, guys, my friends are here, come meet them!
They're pretty excited. I told them all about you guys!
These are my friends-
Leo-
Plitch-
Shari-
Hugh-
and Ruki.
'Sup.
Whoa.
Hi!
Do you notice anything about them?
Yeah, they're like really cool versions of us!
Totally.

Hey, Lilly! You and your friends can sit with us.
Thanks, Gaiana.
Are all of you guys vegetarian?
Pretty much.
Why?
I don't eat meat because I love animals.
My body can only process plants for food.
The environment on my planet can't sustain enough animals for eating.
Bill, you're vegetarian now, too?
Is it because it takes less time to cook?
No, Gammy's vegetarian dishes taste better than the tongue and eyeball meat plates.
It tastes good?
No, just better.

HEPTADAY

At first, we were all intimidated by the other kids from Ossus. We played some soccer and they were all awesome. Some of them are even better than Lilly! Then, they sat in on our math class and ~~apasently~~ apparently are way ahead of us because they already knew all the equations we were working on. They weren't jerks about it, though. And we realized there were some things we do better, too. We were writing poems in creative writing class, and even they knew some of what they wrote was pretty bad. Cronah tried to make fun of them, but they just laughed <u>with</u> him.

I tried to lift a rock with the Force, but smelled a sock, of course.

That's the coolest thing about them—they know they aren't the best at everything, but don't worry about it. They just ~~concintrate~~ concentrate on what they do well. And they all work together, instead of trying to beat one another at everything.

← totally annoyed

How'd you get that shade of blue on your lightsaber, Roan? Mine keeps turning muddy yellow.

YEAR OF THE VISITORS ENDS

Jedi Academy was even more crowded last week as students from the Ossus Campus visited the Coruscant Campus, which was already crowded with visiting Jedi professors. Fortunately, long lines for the bathroom were infrequent and the biggest problem seemed to be Jedi and Padawans stepping on one another's robes. Master Yoda was happy with the visit, declaring, "the merrier, the more! Heh heh." Mr. Garfield was less excited. "Hmph, don't we have enough kids getting into our stuff?" he asked Master Yoda. "Harumph," he added once the visitors left.

Ewok Pilot

By Roan Novachez

I'm surprised how well Ewok Pilot is handling the visit from Jawa Pilot's friends.

I'd say so.

Bont!
Bom'loo!

That's my starship, not Ewok Pilot's, isn't it?
I'd say so.

THE PADAWAN OBSERVER Vol. MXIV #7

Bill, you got a new outfit?
Oh, yeah.
I spilled some of Gammy's cooking on my old outfit, and you know those stains never come out.
Hey, guys.
Nice new outfit, Egon!
This? Oh, yeah, my old robes had a big hole in them.
Hey, guys!
New outfit?
Yeah, my Mom just happened to send this to me...
I see all of you are wearing Ossus style robes. Me, too!
Aren't we cool?
I'm going to go change clothes.
Me, too.
Yep.

Hey, Roan.
What is it, Ronald?
Let me see your answers to the Jedi mind tricks take-home quiz.
No.
I just want to compare...
No, Ronald.
You will show me your answers to the take-home quiz.
Are you trying to use a Jedi mind trick on me?
Er, no... but you WILL show me your answers to the take-home quiz.
You don't need to see my answers to the take-home quiz.
I don't need to see your answers to the take-home quiz.
Hey! What are you two smiling about?

QUADDAY

This year so far has been great. Gaiana might actually be my girlfriend! Pasha laughed at me, because we were talking and I said I wasn't sure if Gaiana and I were really dating, or just good friends hanging out. He and Bill pointed out all the things Gaiana and I do, which made me sound silly.

1. Hold hands

2. Share blue milkshakes

3. Stare at each other for hours

4. Basically do everything together

But I'm nervous, because whenever I think everything is good is usually when I mess stuff up. Even when I'm trying hard to do everything right, I goof up or someone else (like CRONAH) trips me up. Every year I've been at Jedi Academy, something has gone horribly wrong!

This year it'll probably be my independent study with Mr. G. Yesterday he was teaching me about connecting cables, but when I did it there was a loud "BOOM" and all the lights went out. So I blow something up every year, too.

ARC-17… RD SAFETY

Hey, Ro!
Great to hear you and Gaiana are hanging out so much. I'm happy for you! I know Mr. G. is still giving you a hard time, so here's the safety instructions from an ARC-170 to help with your studies. Write back when you're not busy with your GIRLFRIEND! -Dav

Mak… …e buckles tigh… …n case of crash.

In the event of ejection into outer space, DO NOT scream. No one will hear you, and you cannot breathe in space.

Hey, Roan. I'm going to go meet Shi-Fara.
I'll come with you.
She's doing some focus training with Master M'Ba-Tee.
What's her focus, anyway?
Multitasking.
Hi, Pasha! Hi, Roan! I'll be done in a few minutes.
Bew!
Bew!
Have you figured out what you're focusing on for individual training?
Not yet.
Principal Mar told me I should keep meditating about it.
Maybe that could be your focus-meditation!
HMMM...
What's Pasha doing?
His homework.

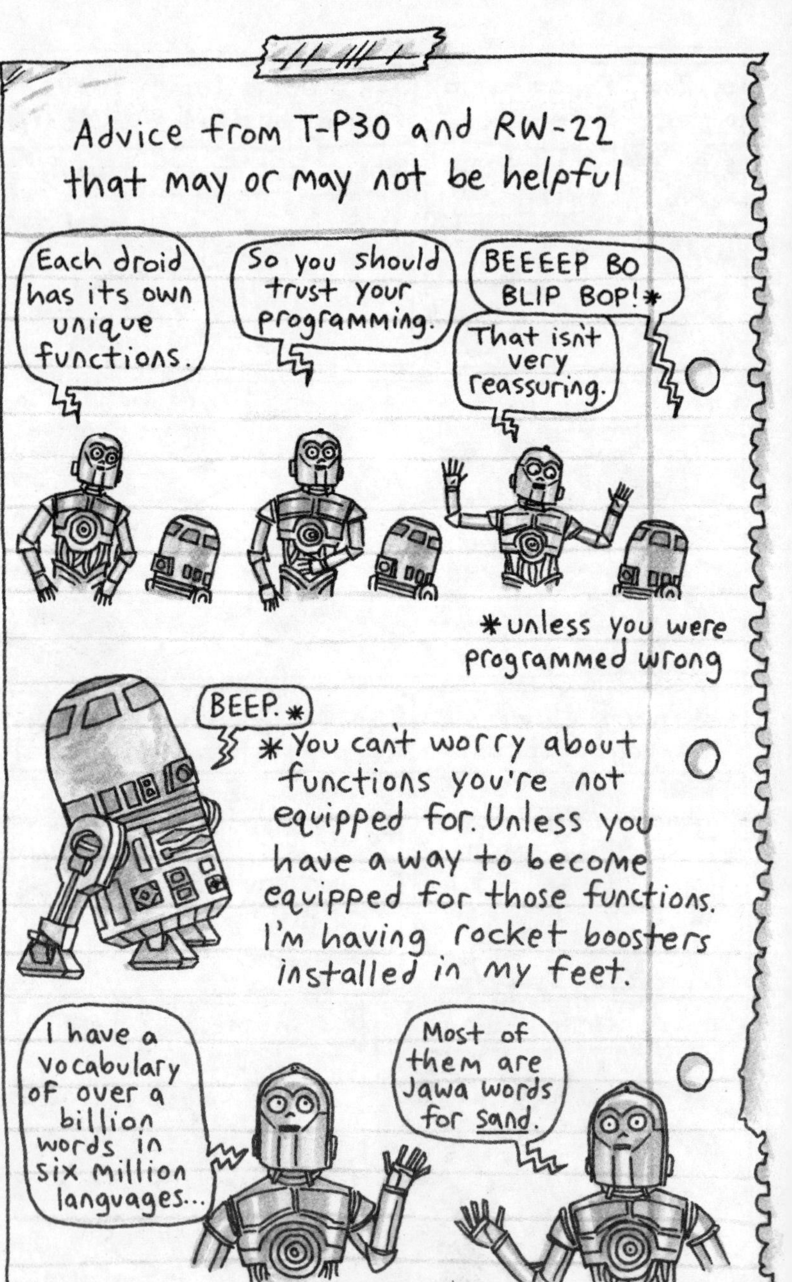
Advice from T-P30 and RW-22 that may or may not be helpful
Each droid has its own unique functions.
So you should trust your programming.
BEEEEP BO BLIP BOP!*
That isn't very reassuring.
*unless you were programmed wrong
BEEP.*
*You can't worry about functions you're not equipped for. Unless you have a way to become equipped for those functions. I'm having rocket boosters installed in my feet.
I have a vocabulary of over a billion words in six million languages...
Most of them are Jawa words for sand.

JEDI ACADEMY TALENT SHOW

Start preparing now! What's your secret ability? Share yours with your fellow Padawans at the Jedi Academy Talent Show!

- Use the Force (if you want to).
- You will have 5 minutes maximum. If you are not done, loud annoying music will start playing until you leave the stage.
- No smoke, fire, or pyrotechnics please.
- Have fun, and don't be afraid of being embarrassed!*
- For A/V needs, contact Bill as soon as possible.
- Grand Prize: Replica Jedi Medallion, presented by Ronald Rinzler, Student Council President and emcee.

* By appearing in the Talent Show, you consent to having your performance holorecorded and posted to Holobook.

MONODAY

I know Jedi are supposed to be prepared for all kinds of situations, but how often will seven-foot-tall Wookiees toss us through the air at lightsaber-wielding foes? Because that was today's class exercise.

Another fun game: Guess Who is More Terrified!

The weird thing is that even though it sounds CRAZY (okay, it IS crazy), when we did the exercise all of our Jedi training kicked in. No one even got hurt, except Greer. But that happened when we were doing our warm-up stretches, so it doesn't count. We had to train extra-hard, too, because we're going on an overnight trip and won't have regular classes for a couple days. Master Yoda was inspired by the Ossus students' visit, so he wants us to stay in downtown Coruscant. I bet the guest Jedi mentors actually thought of it, because they want a break.

You have the rest of the day to explore, but stay with your assigned groups! Meet at the hotel at 1800.
What group are you?
Three.
I'm Two.
Group Two? Hey, Roan, just like old times!
Really?
Where should we go?
The Galactic Museum is this way.
Ugh, no way. BORING.
Look! The Holonet News is filming over there.
Let's get on the news!
C'mon, guys.
Let's go this way.

Let's mess around in some shops.
No, let's go back. We're not supposed to be this far from the hotel.
But you have to stay with your group, Roan.
Afraid you'll get in trouble? Or just afraid?
HMPH.
Shhh!
That was Mr. G.!
You're so scared you're hearing things!
No, I know that "Hmph"! Hide!
HMPH.
It IS Mr. G.!
Shh!
He's coming this way!
SPACE JUNK
Must... not... breathe...
Phew!
You worry too much, Roan.
Can we go now?
Don't you want to shop? This is the kind of junk at your house, right?

HEXADAY

Yesterday sucked because I was stuck with Cronah all day and didn't get to take any of the notes I was supposed to. We didn't even do anything interesting, but Cronah was acting like he was cool. Pasha and Gaiana are way cooler, and they don't even try. Maybe they're cooler BECAUSE they don't try?

I still try, because every time I just try to be myself, I look ridiculous. I should listen to Master Yoda, and try not. Today we switched groups, and I joined up with Pasha, Gaiana, and Tegan. We went to CoCoTown, which sounds like a kids' playground, but is actually the Collective Commerce District. It's full of "exclusive" stores, that just sell stuff you can buy at other stores for less. Themed diners are also popular there, so we made a game of trying to visit as many as possible. We gave up by the time we got to the third one. It's way more fun being with a group that feels like a team.

Starship-themed diner

Ewok-themed diner

Hutt-themed diner

Oops!
Hey!
Watch out!
Sorry, Roan!
KICK!
KICK!
KICK!
SNAP!
I'm so tired of Cronah. I should do something.
I'm going to get him. I'm going to—
Heh heh!
Showing restraint, you are, hm? Use your anger, you do not. Like a Jedi, you act!
Thanks, Master Yoda!
Heh.

Quit copying my answers, Ronald!
I'm not copying you, don't be ridiculous. Look!
You're totally copying! That's my essay question answer in the same words!
Maybe you should change your answer.
Maybe I should tell Master Yoda that you're cheating.
You mean, tell him that YOU'RE cheating?
Huh?
I have the evidence right here in this holorecording.
Hm, looks like you copying my essay answer, Roan.

TRIDAY

Not only do I have Cronah and Mr. G. out to get me, but now *Ronald* is starting to annoy me more than ever. The worst part is the way he cheats. He makes it pretty impossible to get him in trouble. He's a total slimeball. Maybe he's not an actual slimeball, but I still have the urge to wash my hands every time he talks to me. Even when he seems like he's being an okay guy, he's slimy. He apologized to me for cheating (again, since it's not the first time). He said he's trying to be better, but it's hard when everyone else is so much smarter than him. He's just looking for ways to not have to work hard. I think deep down inside he believes that he's the one who's smarter than everyone else. At least he's not as bad as Cronah...

Roan, will you autograph this Ewok Pilot? I'm scrapbooking all your comic strips.
I'm a big fan!
Er, okay.

What are you guys doing?
We're training Voorpee for the talent show.
Watch.
Here you go, Voorpee!
CHOMP!
Cool!
What are you doing for the talent show, Silva?
Uh, I don't know.
I know what you could do...
Ready?
This'll be awesome, right?
I don't know about this...
CRASH!
Maybe not...
Oof!

Here you go, Voorpee, I'll see you tomorrow.

Roan! Are you taking care of Voorpee?
Yeah, why?
I just saw him in the chemistry lab!

Voorpee! How did you escape?

Back into your home you go!

Roan! I just saw Voorpee in the cafeteria!
Hunh?

Okay, all locked up. Stay here, Voorpee!

Roan! Did you leave Voorpee on the soccer field?

How could Voorpee have gotten that far so fast?! It's impossible!

I JUST put him in his cage!
Which was double-locked!

Hey, Roan, Voorpee is loose in the gym. You better go get him.

TRIDAY

Cronah's newest prank is the worst! He kept letting Voorpee out of his cage, and moving him all over the place. So I ended up spending half of today tracking down Voorpee. I don't know how Cronah did it. Maybe he's actually gotten smarter. Or someone is helping him. I would think Cyrus was pulling off the prank with Cronah, but Cyrus has been acting different this year. Maybe he's only pretending to be nice so Lilly likes him.

Let me get the door for you!
Uh, thanks.
Flinch
Flinch

Blah blah blah blah blah!

She must not realize how mean he can be. Unless it's not an act and Cyrus really has come back from the dark side! I tried to talk to Master Yoda about Cronah, but he was busy training Cyrus. Even if I thought it would help, I couldn't talk to Mr. G., either, because Ronald was talking with him for almost an hour. Well, it was more Ronald talking to Mr. G., because all I heard Mr. G. saying was "Hmph."

When I did finally talk to him, Mr. G. gave me a speech about how he'd been expecting me to watch Voorpee more carefully this year, and he didn't want to listen to my explanation of what happened. What's frustrating is that I already expect a lot of myself, and I didn't need Mr. G. lecturing me. I'm putting a lot of pressure on myself because I want this to be the best year ever, but it was easier when I was new and everyone as~~um~~ed assumed I was going to fail. Not everyone, because Pasha and Gaiana have always been really helpful and believed in me. I'm lucky to have them as friends because without them, I probably would fail. I just need to survive having Mr. G. as a teacher.

Ow! You dropped a rock on my foot!
Sorry! Ha ha!
It's okay, you're new! Ha ha!
THE GOOD OLD DAYS!

Chyasse?
Kurruzza, eyeta!
They're becoming a good team. I think they're actually going to fix that.
You do realize they break more stuff as a team, don't you?

holochat ▸ roan_pilot17 .... bigDavN

Hey, Dav, how's it flying?

Good, Ro, how's the Academy for Force-talented kids?

It's okay. I just feel worried a lot...

Why? Are you getting bad grades?

No, I'm even doing okay in my independent study with Mr. G.

Is it Gaiana? She didn't dump you already, did she?

What? No, things with her are great. [and why would she dump me??]

So what's to worry about? Are Cronah and Cyrus still out to get you?

Cronah is, yeah. I'm not sure about Cyrus.

There you go! What you're feeling is just normal, growing-up anxiety.

So even you've felt like this?

Me? Of course not, but I'm special. You're just totally normal.

Roan, that was sweet of you and your friends to send Ollie the backpack. He even took it to bed!
Love, Mom

I lov
My bakpak
Thanc U

I put my buks
in it

JEDI ACADEMY TALENT SHOW PERFORMANCE ORDER

- Please know which act you follow. Be ready to start as soon as the act before you is on stage. Remember, all acts must be 5 minutes or less.
- Keep this handout handy for reference.

01. OPENING REMARKS: Ronald Rinzler ← Hopefully, he talks for <u>less</u> than 5 minutes!

02. JO-AHN: Shadow hand puppets

03. SHI-FARA: Yo-yo tricks

04. TEGAN AND BILL: Music and dance recital

05. ROAN AND GAINA: Voorpak tricks
↑ Ugh, nice typo, whoever typed this up. It's Gai<u>a</u>na.

06. CYRUS: Hula-hoop ← what?

07. MARY: Poetry slam ← what?!!

08. CRONAH: Stand-up comedy routine
↑ Is it comedy if Cronah is the only one laughing?

09. INTERMISSION

Next up we have Tegan and Bill with a music and dance recital.
Are you nervous?
No.
I was asking Voorpee.
Merp!
Just kidding.
Are you nervous?
Yes, but I'm pretending not to be.
CLAP CLAP CLAP CLAP CLAP CLAP CLAP CLAP CLAP CLAP CLAP CLAP
CLAP CLAP CLAP
That's our signal!
Now Roan and Gaiana will perform with the trained voorpak, Voorpee.

All right, Voorpee... jump!
Roan, what are you doing?
It's Voorpee... I don't know!
Annnnd... jump!
Let's try something else...
Okay, Voorpee, roll over!
Aaahh! Roan!
HOP!
Oh!
He's peeing on me!
Ha ha! That's all for Roan and Gaiana, heh...
Next up, we have Cyrus, with his hula-hoops!
That was the WORST!!

I'm sorry, Gaiana! I don't know what's going on with Voorpee.
Here, take him! I've never been so embarrassed...
In front of the whole school!...
Voorpee, are you feeling okay? What's wrong?
mer?
HEY!
Another Voorpee?!
CRASH!
OUCH!!
Oh, no!
Wait!
There can't be TWO Voorpees!
Eek! Voorpee is loose under here!
Roan, get your voorpak!

AIEEE!
It's on my head!
IT'S ON MY HEAD!
Eeek!
WHAT'S GOING ON, NOVACHEZ?!
You don't want to know.

QUADDAY

The talent show was attacked by hundreds of Voorpees! One jumped on Cyrus, and he fell and broke his arm. They had to cancel the rest of the show while we caught all the Voorpees. The worst part was

that everyone was annoyed at <u>ME</u> because they thought it was my fault! It wasn't Voorpee, though. It was clones of Voorpee. I'm sure Cronah isn't smart enough to clone voorpaks, but he must have known about it. I don't know anyone else who would want to play a prank like that on me. And Voorpee! At least Principal Mar decided to let us finish the talent show the next day in the gym. Cronah had extra time to prepare his stand-up comedy, so he came up with a lot of jokes about Gaiana and me. Really, it was all the same joke, and it wasn't

Either Roan and Gaiana break up, or they're going to break <u>us</u>!
Whoa!

even funny the first time he made a "break" joke. Let's see... he said something about Cyrus needing to take a break, that he thought the phrase was "break a leg" not "break an arm," that maybe Tegan could do some break-dancing, something about spring break... soooo annoying. Cyrus wasn't even that upset about his arm getting broken, even though the school bacta tanks are under ~~Maitenance~~ Maintenance and he has to wear a sling and cast on his arm until after spring break. I think he's enjoying the attention, especially from Lilly. I still felt like it was partly my fault, so I was glad Gaiana didn't stay upset. She was more worried about taking care of all the voorpaks. I can't wait for spring break, because this whole semester has been an almost space-train wreck. OF COURSE someone is out to get me as soon as I stop messing things up on my own.

Actual funniest act in the talent show

Roan, you're good at art. Will you draw on my cast?

STUDENT: ROAN NOVACHEZ	
LEVEL: PADAWAN	SEMESTER: FIVE
JEDI MENTOR: MR. GARFIELD	
REPORT CARD	

CLASS	NOTES	GRADE
HABITS OF USING THE FORCE [MASTER YODA]	Good! Realize he was using the Force, Roan sometimes did not!	A
PRACTICAL MATH [MRS. PILTON]	Roan knows all of his numbers, they just don't always add up for him.	B
CREATIVE WRITING [LIBRARIAN LACKBAR]	Roan's writing is always humorous, with delightful drawings!	A
ETHICS OF JEDI MIND TRICKS [PRINCIPAL MAR]	ROAN HAS ABILITY BUT LACKS PROPER CONTROL.	B-
INDEPENDENT STUDY I [MR. GARFIELD]	ROAN DID WELL, BUT COULD STILL STUDY MORE INDEPENDENTLY.	A-
LIGHTSABER ACROBATICS [KITMUM AND MR. GARFIELD]		
ADVANCED STAR PILOT TRAINING [MR. GARFIELD]	NEEDS TO FINISH MAKEUP ASSIGNMENTS FOR A FINAL GRADE.	INC.- INCOMPLETE

Bye, Roan!
Bye! Good luck getting the voorpak clones to Naboo!
Shouldn't you be going with the voorpaks, Roan?
We both know it wasn't my fault, Cronah.
No, but you belong in a zoo.
Have a good break, Cronah.
If you were in a zoo, I'd visit you, Roan!
Ha, thanks, Pasha.
Bye, Roan! Bye, Pasha!
Bye, Lilly! Uh... sorry about your arm, Cyrus.
It's okay. See ya later.

Was Lilly carrying Cyrus's bag?
Well, yeah. He does have a broken arm.

Plus they're definitely dating.
Definitely.

So, what are you doing for spring break?
I need to figure out my focus before I come back.

But my family will be camping the whole time. It's going to be fun.
What are you doing?

HOMEWORK.
Oh, right.

Have a good break, Mr. Garfield.
HMPH.

That was nice. He was actually happy.
You're being sarcastic, right?
No, I've learned to distinguish his different "hmphs."

HEPTADAY

The first half of this year went by SO fast. I was so busy, they must have been giving us more homework this year. Actually, I still have homework to do, even though it's break, because of all my work getting ruined when SOMEONE took my backpack, who I will not name, except to say that it was totally CRONAH. So my spring break will only be partly a break. At least I have an excuse to not have to work in the garden here as much. Jedi Academy spring breaks have never gone well for me. So far I had one where I just did chores and sat around bored, one where I almost lost my best friend, and now one where I'm just doing homework. Still, I get to hang out with Ollie and Dav, and Dad will be home in a couple days.

I think Ewok Pilot might need a break.
zzzzzzzz

Roan, you are Jedi Master!

I wish!

snore
OOF!
ROAN! ROAN! Wake up!
BOUNCE
BOUNCE
Yawn.
Will you play with me?
okay.
I wish I could use the Force in my sleep...
Let's go! Let's go!
You're it!
Bew! Bew!
Wheeeee!
Haha!
Roan, I know it's spring break, but you can't sleep ALL day. Why don't you play with your brother?

Hey, Roan. Still stuck pretending those rocks are spaceships?
Hunh?
No, this is my daily Jedi meditation exercise.
I'm supposed to randomly arrange the rocks, then contemplate any meaningful patterns I see.
Ha! Your school is so weird!
Yeah. Sometimes I do pretend the rocks are spaceships, though.
Whoa!
That's cool.

TRIDAY

I'm glad Dav and Dad got here in time to help me with my homework. Of course, they still made me do it all myself, but they both checked it and made sure I wasn't making any huge mistakes. It's not so much that it took less time, I just felt less ~~anxhus~~ anxious and stressed about getting all the work done. We did have time to do something as a family, even if it was just visiting the Museum of Tatooine in Bestine. It was a lot of fun, a little bit because I hadn't visited there in a long time, but mostly because Ollie had NEVER been there. He was so excited, I thought he was going to pass out!

I think you missed a part of one question.
Where?
On that page.
But where?
Keep looking.
Just tell me!

It's going to eat me! Aaaahh!
ANCIENT KRAYT DRAGON SKULL

holochat ▷roan_pilot17..........g@!@naG

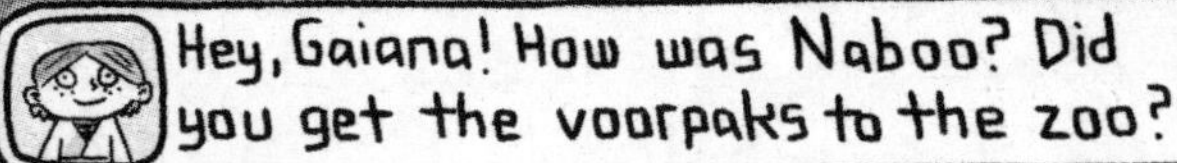

Hey, Gaiana! How was Naboo? Did you get the voorpaks to the zoo?

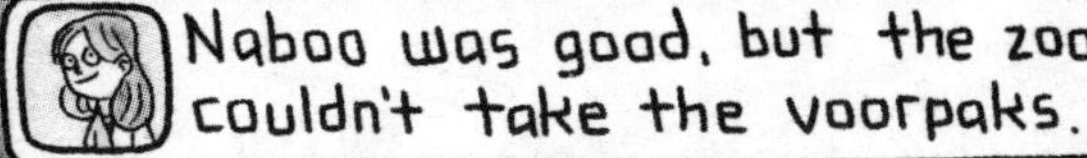

Naboo was good, but the zoo couldn't take the voorpaks.

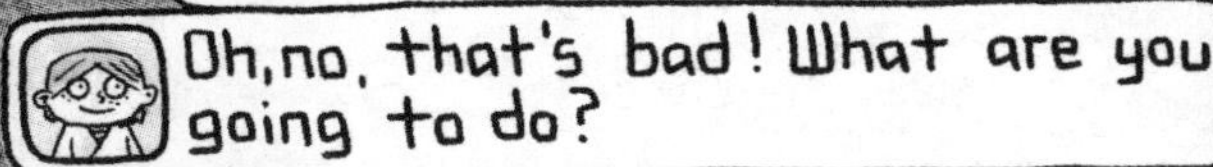

Oh, no, that's bad! What are you going to do?

Fortunately I found a Voorpak Rescue Organization.

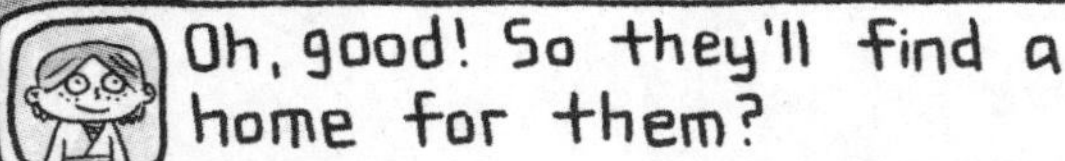

Oh, good! So they'll find a home for them?

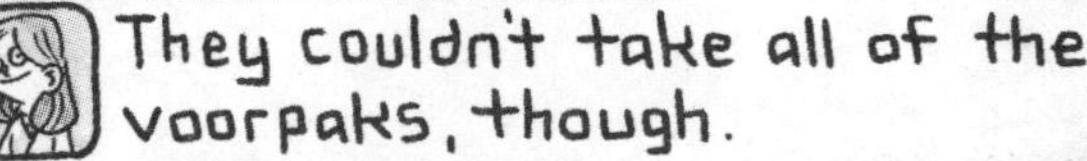

They couldn't take all of the voorpaks, though.

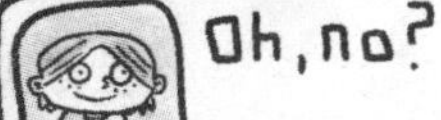

Oh, no?

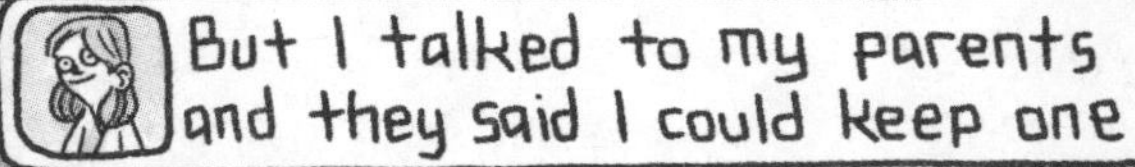

But I talked to my parents and they said I could keep one.

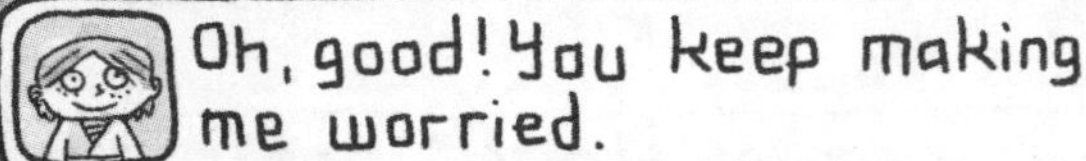

Oh, good! You keep making me worried.

Hee hee, I know! How has your break been?

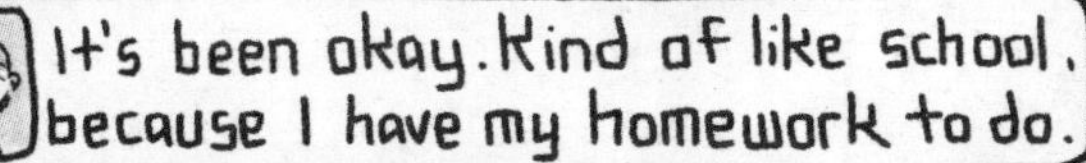

It's been okay. Kind of like school, because I have my homework to do.

I'm sorry. At least if you're caught up, we can hang out more! I miss you.

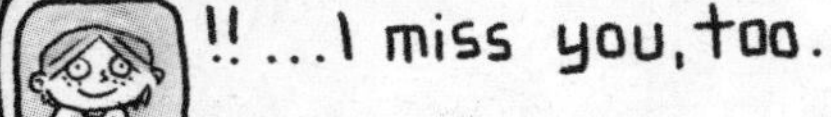

!! ...I miss you, too.

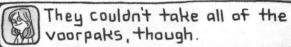

I can't believe spring break is over already.

I didn't even really get a break. Good thing this flight is so long. At least I can relax a little...

BOO!
AIEEEEEEE!

Ha ha ha ha ha ha!
Cronah?! What are you doing on my spacebus?

I had to make special arrangements, but it was totally worth it!

You don't mind if I take my shoes off, do you? This is a pretty long flight. Maybe I'll take a nap... if you hear a loud noise, it's just me snoring.
BURP!
Excuse me, heh!

Gaiana!
little wave
Um, how are you?
Are you okay?
I'm embarrassed.
What? Why?
I got braces.
My brother Dav had braces. You don't need to be embarrassed.
Hey, Gaiana, did you eat a droid?
Unless Cronah sees me.
Unless Cronah sees you.
Ha ha!

STUDENT: ROAN NOVACHEZ

LEVEL: PADAWAN | SEMESTER: SIX

HOMEROOM: MASTER YODA

CLASS SCHEDULE

0730-0850: RECKONING WITH THE FORCE

Master Yoda will teach students how to reckon with forces to be reckoned with by using the Force.

0900-0950: PUZZLE SOLVING

Students will use logic and creativity to study problem solving with Mrs. Pilton.

1000-1050: CLASSICS OF GALACTIC LITERATURE

Librarian Lackbar will guide the students in reading important books they should've read already.

1100-1150: INDEPENDENT STUDY II

Students will continue intense, individual studies with their Jedi mentors.

1200-1300: LUNCH BREAK

1300-1350: PRINCIPLES OF LIGHTSABER DEFENSE

Mr. Garfield will instruct students on parries, counterattacks, and other lightsaber defenses.

1400-1450: SENTIENT SPECIES COMMUNICATIONS

Principal Mar will show students how to communicate with species that mumble

1500-1550: EXTREME JEDI GYMNASTICS

Students will risk embarrassment, injury, and pain to learn difficult new moves with Kitmum.

PENTADAY

I was surprised to see Gaiana when I got back here, because she never said anything to me about getting braces, but it's because she feels embarrassed. I told her that, considering how often I do something awkward and embarrassing, she'll be lucky if anyone notices her braces.

Mostly, I bet she's worried about kids like Cronah. So hopefully he just keeps picking on me. If he's going to pick on anyone, at least. I wonder when he's going to stop paying so much attention to me and start worrying about himself. He's always putting other people down to make himself look better, even though half the time he doesn't really look any better. If anything, he looks like a bigger jerk.

Stuff Kitmum Growled
This Week That
Didn't Make Sense
GROWARGHH!*
RAOWRRR!**
AROORRRAHRW!***
*The best thing is
being the best!
**Being the best doesn't
mean there isn't someone
better.
***So the best thing
is being better
than the best!
GROWARLL REOWRR
AWORLL WORRA!*
*Just because you're not
the best at what you do
doesn't mean you should
do something else, because
maybe what you do is
what you're best at
doing.
RAOWAR!*
*The best
defense
is a good
offense.
GREOWWR?*
*I don't
know what
the best
offense
is, though.

Hmph. Do you even want to be a pilot, Roan?
What?! Yes!
Why?
Uh, because I've always wanted to?
But why have you always wanted to?
Is this a trick question?
Hmph. Yes.
Oh, ha ha!
Now I want you to write an essay answering my trick question.
Is that a trick, too?
No.
Hey, Roan. How was studying with Mr. G. today?
Okay. How was studying with Librarian Lackbar?
It's great! We spend a lot of time talking, she helps me work through problems, I get lots of positive feedback..
I have no idea what that's like.

WHY I WANT TO BE A PILOT
By Roan Novachez

GLAD YOU'RE FINALLY THINKING ABOUT THIS.
A-

My dad is a pilot, so ever since I was a little kid, I wanted to be a pilot like him and my brother. The first time I flew in a starship, I was four years old and my dad let me steer. Not really, but he let me hold on like I was steering, and that was the coolest, best feeling I've ever had.

My friends and I always practiced on flight simulators in elementary school, and I was always one of the top students. My dad gets to help a lot of people as a pilot. Even service pilots are pretty helpful, so if I become a really good pilot I can help a lot of people, too. Besides, Tatooine is hot and boring, and I'm not good at farming. So I want to be a pilot.

DUODAY

The more I work with Mr. G., the weirder he seems. I'm not sure what difference it makes to him <u>WHY</u> I want to be a pilot? It's just one of those teacher things where they want you to think about something, but they don't tell you how it's supposed to help you. I'm sure this is just his way of messing with me. Like the other day, he told me I was going to fly the simulator for a transport escort exercise, but it was actually a space station docking exercise. So I studied the wrong manual and kept crashing. Then Mr. G. also tells me I'm making a lot of progress. He won't tell me what grade I'm on track to get, though. He just tells me, "Hmph, don't worry about it."

A crash-landing is just a crash, not a landing.
Hmph.

Which makes me worry about it even more. At least my other training is going well. Maybe I'll become the first Jedi starship mechanic.

One of many tools for a Jedi, the Force is. Heh heh!

RAORRR!
We have to get past this without using the Force?!
This is impossible.
Ha! You guys need to use your brains.
We can just go AROUND this.
RAOWRR!!
Yipe!
Most impressive, Ronald.
Kitmum helped.
You went the wrong way.

Stuff Yoda Said This Week
Judge a book by its cover, do you?
What is inside, a good book makes, hm?
Hmmm. Boring, sometimes the inside of a book is, too.
Decide, you must, what you want to be.
Also, be what you want to be, you must be.
If perfect you try to be, forever will it consume you. Perfect, nothing is!

Roan, can you help me? I need to print my paper, but it's not working.
Sure!
It's due tomorrow, so I want to be all done so we can hang out after class today.
Hm, let's see. Just click this and this, and there we go.
TAK TAK
It's not printing.
Yeah, see?
These are all plugged in...
Did you try resetting all of the settings?
Yeah.
Reboot the programs?
Yep.
Reconfigure the configurations?
I re-re'ed everything.

Maybe we should wait and find Librarian Lackbar.
Let me try one more thing...
Uh, which file was yours?
What do you mean?
Where's my file?!
Isn't it...
TAK TAK TAK TAK
Oh, no!
I didn't move it.
Did you re-save it?
I thought I did.
I'm going to have to re-write the whole thing!
That was the one re-re thing you didn't try yet, at least?
Just move, so I can do this.
I'm sorry.
Can you just go away, please?
She thinks it's totally my fault.
TAK
TAK
TAK
TAK
TAK
TAK

QUADDAY

I'm very confused. I thought Gaiana was REALLY angry at me, because we were supposed to hang out yesterday, but after I may (or may not) have deleted her whole paper, she didn't want to hang out. At least, that's what I assumed, because she was all "I can't hang out with you now," and acted super-distracted. Then she didn't sit by me for breakfast. Well, she didn't sit by anyone, because she didn't come to breakfast before class, but still. Then, today after class, I was ready to make it up to her. I drew a little apology note, and got her a holodata backup to use, but before I even gave those to her, she was happy to see me and wanted to hang out. I didn't realize that even Jedi can be confused by the opposite gender...

What Gaiana says →
I can't hang out with you.
I need your help.
I'm not angry with you.
I don't know what happened.
What she means? →
Let's hang out!
I don't need your help.
I'm just really annoyed.
What did you do?

Almost there...
OBJECTIVE REACHED
TIME 04:29s
DAMAGE 0.032%
BONUSES +127
MISSION COMPLETE
Good work, Roan.
Here it comes.
That was nearly flawless.
But... let me guess.
I managed to get minimal damage, but took longer than my best time record.
I missed over a dozen bonus points.
And my helmet strap was one level of tightness off of regulation.
You can always do better, of course, but don't let that take away from what you accomplish.
Who are you and what did you do with Mr. G.?

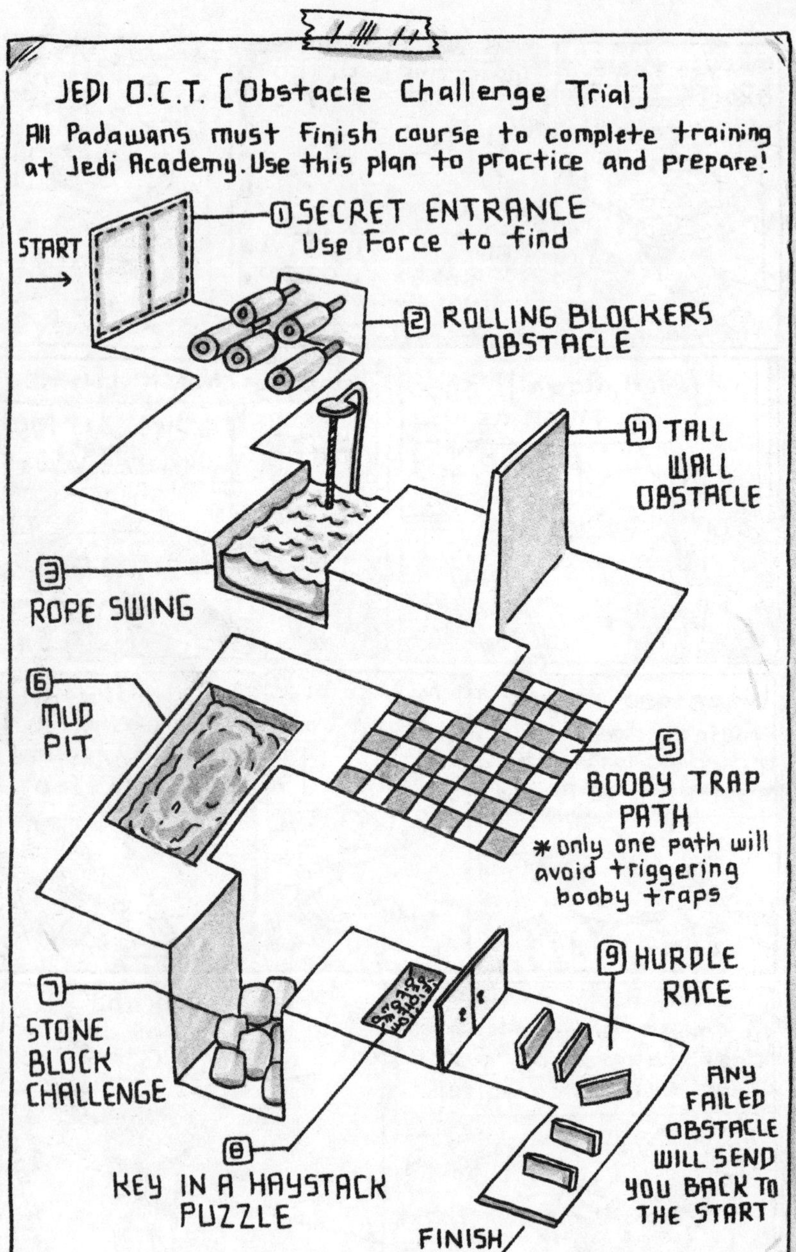
JEDI O.C.T. [Obstacle Challenge Trial]
All Padawans must finish course to complete training at Jedi Academy. Use this plan to practice and prepare!
START
1 SECRET ENTRANCE
Use Force to find
2 ROLLING BLOCKERS OBSTACLE
3 ROPE SWING
4 TALL WALL OBSTACLE
5 BOOBY TRAP PATH
* only one path will avoid triggering booby traps
6 MUD PIT
7 STONE BLOCK CHALLENGE
8 KEY IN A HAYSTACK PUZZLE
9 HURDLE RACE
ANY FAILED OBSTACLE WILL SEND YOU BACK TO THE START
FINISH

Okay, guys, tell me what to expect from this Obstacle Challenge Trial.
We've never had to do this before.
You actually know as much as us!
I finally caught up with you guys!
And it only took you three years!
We've been doing most of this with Kitmum...
Yeah, but we thought extra training couldn't hurt, so we set up our own course.
Ha!
Who's first?
I'll go!

JUMP!
BOUNCE!
LEAP!
As long as there are couches on the course, it'll be easy!
Land!
Roan, you go next.
Oops!
HOP!
BOUNCE!
OOF!
Are you okay?!
I thought extra training couldn't hurt?! I REALLY hope there are couches...

HEPTADAY

I thought I was going to be au~~tomat~~icly automatically prepared for the physical part of the Obstacle Challenge Trial. Everyone else made practice look easy. As soon as I stop focusing, though, I mess up right away. It's not that I can't do it, or even that I'm not good at that stuff, but I just need to pay attention and work at it. I bet the mental side of it will be easier.

I've always been good at puzzles and games. I'm one of the best players at holochess. Too bad my brain isn't a muscle or something.

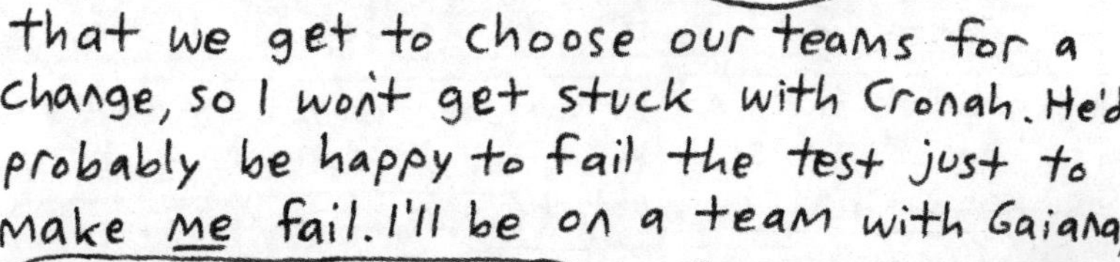

Nice move, Roan!
Blush

The exciting thing is that we get to choose our teams for a change, so I won't get stuck with Cronah. He'd probably be happy to fail the test just to make ME fail. I'll be on a team with Gaiana, Pasha, and Shi-Fara. Being on a team with them makes me a lot less worried about passing this test.

Will learning how to do a somersault really make them better pilots?
Probably not, but them seem to enjoy it.
Utinni!
Yub yub!

Hey, Roan! Can I ask you something?
Yeah, sure.
What was that defensive move you used in your lightsaber duel last year?
When Pasha attacked from above?
You block like this...
...then swing up to try and catch your opponent off guard.
Oh, yeah. Thanks for showing me.
No problem.
It's good to have a plan for defense, you know what I mean?
Uh, yeah.
I have no idea what he means.
If someone is out to get you, you should be ready to defend, got it?
Yeah, totally.
Is he trying to warn me, or threaten me?

REMINDER
Students must have Space Pox vaccinations up to date this year.
*not actual size

JOIN US FOR AN ICE CREAM SOCIAL
All-natural ice cream made by the students!
On The Jedi Academy Front Lawn. Pentaday

PLEASE DO NOT PLACE ICE CREAM ON TOP OF DROIDS

OPENS NEXT HEXADAY
CORUSCANT GALLERY OF MODERN ART
KEFF D'IRST
EXHIBITION OF NEW ARTWORKS

EWOK PILOT

By Roan Novachez

You two have to patrol while my spaceship is being repaired.
Mambay.
Acha.

Na goo!
Sabioto!

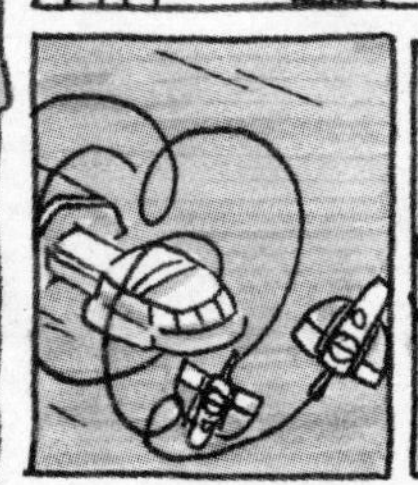

BOOM!

The good news is they stopped the space pirates.
They're back? Where are their starships?

THE PADAWAN OBSERVER Vol. MXIV #9

Roan, you're in the Cooking Club?
No, Shi-fara needed a break, so I'm helping out.
Thanks for helping, Roan!
You're welcome!
What's wrong?
Does yours taste... funny?
I don't know yet...
Is it your braces?
Roan, what did you do to this ice cream?! It tastes like... worm intestines...
Ugh!
I'm gonna be sick!
plop
crunch crunch
Are these crunchy bits legs? Insect legs?!

I didn't make it, I was just scooping it out for people!
Roan, how did Voorpee's insect pet food get in the ice cream?! You were supposed to be watching!
I don't know, I was just scooping, and...
That's odd, my ice cream tastes fine, Roan.
I don't think this is Roan's fault.
Cronah!
Don't worry, we can open up a new batch.
Sorry if a bunch is getting wasted.
It's not a total waste. Gammy loves it!
URMM!

MONODAY

AAAAAARRRRRGGGGGHHHHH!!! If Jedi aren't supposed to give in to their frustration, can they at least write about it? This SHOULD be the best year of Jedi Academy Middle School, and basically it is, but Cronah is keeping it from being perfect. HE IS ALWAYS MESSING WITH ME. Of course he doesn't admit to anything, and I can't prove it. At the Ice Cream Social, someone poured mite sauce and beetle jelly and other gross stuff into the ice cream (when I happened to be scooping it). RW-22 also identified fish, radish, and insect paste in the ice cream. If it wasn't Cronah, who was it? No one else has given me a hard time every day since I first got here. Not even Cyrus. I wonder if there'd be a kid just like Cronah at Plant School if I ended up there.

It couldn't have been me, Mr. Garfield. I was over there. I'm training to be a Jedi, not a magician!
HMPH.

Oh, was this your final project, Roan? I thought it was weeds.

CLASSICS OF GALACTIC LITERATURE

✱ Write summaries of 3 books

The Count of Mon Calamari

The story of a Mon Calamari sailor falsely held prisoner on an island by Quarren. Escapes by swimming away and uses analytic skills to plot revenge.

The Call of the Force

Story is about tauntaun named Buck that is rescued from abusive owners by a Jedi on ice planet Hoth.

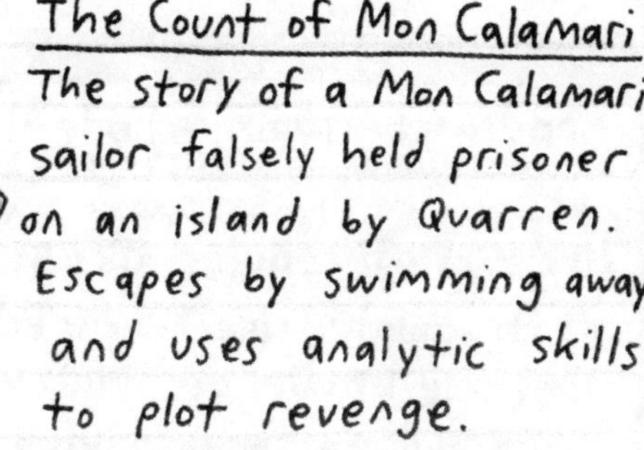

The Golden Widget

Charlie and the Droid Factory

Tells the story of a young Jawa named Charlie who wins a tour of a droid factory and then gets to take over running it.

holomail

FROM: P_Mar
TO: Padawan Class Group
SUBJECT: Obstacle Challenge Trial

OPTIONS
◀ REPLY
▶ FORWARD
■ PRINT
● POST TO HOLOBOOK

Good afternoon, students.

Instead of regular classes tomorrow, all Padawans are required to take the Obstacle Challenge Trial. Each four-student team will have one half hour to complete the course. If you fail an obstacle, your team will need to restart the course. No further guidance will be given regarding how to get past obstacles, so your team will need to figure out the solution for each challenge without help.

May the Force be with you,
Principal Mar

P.S. Failure to complete the O.C.T. will result in having to repeat this year at Jedi Academy. Of course, I have faith that all of you will pass, so you may refrain from worrying.

TRIDAY

I'm getting nervous about the Obstacle Challenge Trial. What if I DO fail, and I have to stay at Jedi Academy another year while everyone else gets to move on? I wasn't stressed about this test before, because it seems pretty easy. I thought maybe that's why you have to repeat the year if you fail, because if you can't do something THAT easy, you're not ready for more Jedi training. Now I'm not sure I AM ready for more Jedi training. Jedi aren't supposed to get nervous, are they? That could be the real test: The teachers want to try and make us nervous so they can tell who doesn't really belong. I should get some sleep now, but I need to stop thinking about tomorrow first.

SECRET ENTRANCE
00:00
Your team's turn it is. May the Force be with you!
Heh heh heh.
Where's the entrance though?
Easy! Here it is.
Gooood... Use the Force, you did?
No, someone from the team before us had muddy shoes.
Oh, heh heh heh!
ROLLING BLOCKERS
03:32
They should really call these "squishers"!
OOF!

ROPE SWING
How do we get the rope?
Use the Force!
8:28
AAAaahoooahhHHH!
TALL WALL
I've got an idea!
Hurry!
Uh-oh!
12:19
We'll catch you!
BOOBY-TRAP PATH
So what path will avoid the traps!
Only one way to find out!
CLICK!
Yikes!
FWIP!
Easy, just don't step on that spot!
Wait!
Or that spot!
CLICK!
FWOOOOSH!
Watch out for this spot, too!
FWOOP!
FWOP!
FWIP
CLICK!
FWOOP!

This isn't so bad!
Very good, hmm.
16:52
MUD PIT
The next challenge should've been a shower.
For the record, I did NOT just have an accident.
20:52
STONE BLOCKS
What do we do here?
Maybe we have to make a bridge out of the stones?
We could use the Force to stack them.
Good idea.
Steady...
That's it...
Focus...
I can't focus when you keep telling me to focus!

26:06
Hurry!
KEY IN A HAYSTACK
We have to find the right key?!
We don't have time to try them all!
Silva showed me something – we can use the Force to feel which key has been used...
This one!
HURDLE RACE
29:33
Let's go!
We're almost out of time!

29:50
Oops!
29:59
OOF!
Huff huff!
Congratulations, hmmm? Well, you have all done!
Phew!
Only one second left!
That was close!
29:59
Close? Second?
29:59
Hmm, fast, that clock runs! Ten minutes you still have left.
Heh heh heh!

PENTADAY

I felt super ~~releived~~ relieved after finishing the Obstacle Challenge Trial. I felt like: I did it! Yes! Awesome! And then I remembered we still have half of a semester left. Everyone ended up passing the test, although Bill's team almost didn't, because Egon got stuck in the mud for a while.

My team had the second best time. Lilly's team finished fastest. She was with Cyrus, Jo-Ahn, and Silva. I was surprised that Silva was on that team instead of Cronah. I thought Cronah might be annoyed that he wasn't on their team, but when his team finished they were all cheering Cronah like he was really great or something, which Cronah LOVED. I just wish I knew why Cronah acts the way he does. He always makes sure to put

Yeah!
Awesome!
REALLY HAPPY TO COME IN THIRD!

down other people, so they don't look as good. That annoys me a lot, because I already know I'm not the best. I'm just happy that I'm doing well enough to not get kicked out or fail. I'd be doing even better if I didn't have to deal with Cronah (allegedly) messing with me. For some reason he's really distracting to me, even when he's not doing anything all that bad. Like, he had a birthday dinner last week, and invited everyone EXCEPT me.

I'm sure he didn't expect everyone to come, but he invited them just so he could NOT give me an invitation. Not that I would've gone. Even Cyrus didn't go. He said he had a lot of work to do for his independent study, but I hope the real reason is that he's finally tired of Cronah being a jerk.

The best birthday card I got last year: (from Dav)

Inside it says: "Please tell the Ewoks not to cook ME for your birthday dinner"

Hey, Roan, we need to take a holopicture of you for the yearbook.
Good thing I wore my clean robes today.
Okay, so—
CLICK Flash!
Uh, can you take another? I think my eyes were closed.
Of course, we always take a couple, just in case.
Oh, good, because—
CLICK Flash!
Gaiana, we can take yours now, too. Let's see that smile!
I can't see now.

holomail

FROM: JA_Yearbook_Staff
TO: roan_pilot17
SUBJECT: Yearbook Photo

OPTIONS
◁ REPLY
▷ FORWARD
□ PRINT
○ POST TO HOLOBOOK

Dear Student,

Congratulations on nearly completing middle school! Please review your yearbook photo choices and personal information. Reply to this holomail with your photo choice, any corrections, and the number of yearbooks you would like to purchase. Remember, yearbooks make great gifts out of great memories!

Name: Roane Novacheeze
Home Planet: Tattooine

HMPH. HRMPH. HUMPH. HMMMMMPH. *
Sweet! I did well.
* "Not bad. Pretty good. Yes. Very good, in fact."
Hmph. I don't see you getting any better, Roan.
Oh.
Do you know why that is?
Um...
Because my scores have been so good?
Yeah, right.
Is he serious?

Good job.
Now what?
That's it. You're pretty Much a pilot.
I wonder if I have time to see if he's serious about that, too...

TRIDAY

When I first got to Jedi Academy, I thought Master Yoda was the most confusing teacher, because I couldn't understand what he was saying. Now Yoda seems completely straightforward and Mr. Garfield is the most confusing. He'll point out everything I'm doing wrong on an assignment, and then tell me "Good job!" But then I'll get every answer right on a quiz and he'll give me a disappointed look and act like I FAILED. So whenever I've started to feel confident that everything is cool, I end up doing worse on a test or paper. Which is maybe what he wants? Like, he's just setting me up so I'll fail. Maybe he's even working <u>with</u> Cronah— except he gives Cronah a hard time, too. Unless <u>that's</u> also part of Mr. G.'s plan! If I knew, then I could try to stop him.

Confused, look, you, hm? Heh heh heh!
ROAN, I'M GOING TO GET YOU!
A NEW HELMET.
THAT ONE LOOKS BIG.

Stuff Yoda Said
This Week
Try not, hmm?
Except new things.
Try new things, you should!
Heh heh heh.
Train yourself to let go...of everything you fear to try.
Hmph. Adventure. Heh. Excitement. A Jedi craves not these things.
But afraid to go on adventures, a Jedi is not!
Strong, am I, with the Force, but not that strong. Heh.
To fly, learn to pilot a starship, I must. Heh!

Roan, what's wrong? You look like a zombie.
Roan got a holomail that said there was training at 0400 this morning.
There was training this morning?
No, it was a prank. The message was from Master YoFa.
If I had read it closely, I would've known. Look.
"Important training, this is." Sounds real.
Keep reading.
"For your butt, this training is. Many farts, you will have."
Giggle!
Poor Roan, I'm sorry! We'll help you get through the day.
Here's a napkin.
SPLAT!

MONODAY

Pasha took so long to decide what he was going to focus on, he has to do some catch-up work. He ended up choosing diplomacy, which to be honest, sounds a little boring. Principal Mar says that sometimes Jedi Knights have to negotiate using their lightsabers. Pasha asked if that didn't make it something other than "negotiating" but Principal Mar didn't answer. So this week Pasha and I practiced a lot of "negotiating." That should help me in the Labyrinth Trial, since lightsaber fencing is a big part of it. I also helped Egon with his studies. He's studying programming–so he actually found a way to make his focus playing video games! He needed a playtester for showing the game he created to his Jedi mentor. I'm not great at video games, but I think it helped.

We probably shouldn't yell "Watch out!" before we attack.

What does this button do? Ooh! What happened? How do I do this?

holomail

FROM: master_yoda_642
TO: Padawan Class Group
SUBJECT: Labyrinth Trial

OPTIONS
◁ REPLY
▷ FORWARD
□ PRINT
○ POST TO HOLOBOOK

For the Labyrinth Trial, helpful, this map will be. Memorize it, you should! Bring it with you, you may not.

May the Force be with you!

- Master Yoda

I wonder if Cronah will try to sabotage me in the Labyrinth Trial...
This is his last chance to get me kicked out!
Or maybe it's too late for me to get kicked out.
Plus I'll have Pasha and Gaiana to help.
Gaiana is so great...
Wait, where am I?
Oh, no, I'm late for class!
Roan, we saw you wandering around practicing for the labyrinth.
Good idea!
Oh, yeah, that's what I was doing.

HEPTADAY

Everyone is starting to freak out about the end of the school year coming up. Shi-Fara spent two hours writing her name, crossing it out, then rewriting it at the top of her puzzle-solving paper. Tegan mixed up all the pages of the new issue of the school newspaper and had to stop the printer and re-do it.

This must be perfect... PERFECT...

And Cyrus has been like a different person. He asked to borrow the combat remote for lightsaber practice. I would've said no, except Lilly was with him, and I felt like I had to say yes or she'd think saying no had something to do with her and not the time that Cyrus and Cronah borrowed it and broke it. This time, Cyrus brought it back in even BETTER condition. Even Gaiana has been acting strange, I think. But maybe not. I've never had a girlfriend before, so how would I know? She kept looking

Thanks, Roan!
I cleaned out the hover sensor and washed the laser filters, too.
Oh, and I recalibrated the circuit levels for you...

all impatient with me, but not about anything in particular. Or she'd ask if I had any plans, or what I was up to later in the week, and then she would elbow me SUPER-HARD!

I don't know, what are you—OOF!

I had no idea what she was talking about until finally she asked me if I would go on a date with her, which is what she wanted ME to ask HER. We've gone on a few double dates, and we're always hanging out, but Shi-Fara explained to me that I hadn't gone on, like, an ACTUAL date with just Gaiana. So we made plans but I got nervous and almost canceled because I felt like I was going to barf, but Pasha made me go and it was AWESOME. We went for a picnic in the woods by the soccer field, which normally we can't go in without special permission, but because Gaiana is studying nature with Librarian Lackbar, we were allowed to. It was the best.

she taught me all about the trees

all by ourselves!

It was a hot day, but perfect in the shade

delicious sandwiches AND brownies

spent most of the time staring at each other and smiling

ADVERTISEMENT

LAST CHANCE! Preorder your class ring now to receive 10% off. Made of high-quality Durasteel!

Cheap plastic version also available

PLEASE TURN in your teacher feedback evaluation form by next week. This will help future students have the best educational experience. Thank you.

EWOK PILOT: UNLEASHED By Roan Novachez

Ewok Pilot, you've achieved top ranking as a pilot. That means you can lead your own flight team.

Congratulations!

Teeha!

I'll miss that guy.

Me, too. Except for him accidentally blowing us up.

I wonder who he'll recruit for his team?

Na-chin treek ota luka!

Yubnub!

Okka!

Yub yub!

Yup yup!

Yun yum!

Ibana!

THE PADAWAN OBSERVER Vol. MXIV #10

HEPTADAY

It wasn't as traumatic as when my backpack was filled with food, but the latest prank played on me was still pretty frustrating. I went back to my dorm room during lunch break and someone had put grease on my door. When I tried to open it, I got grease all over my hands. I tried to wipe my hands off on my clothes but that just got it all over my clothes, too. I still couldn't open the door, because it was too slippery. One of the guest Jedi mentors saw me and let me borrow clothes, which was totally embarrassing. Especially because a bunch of the grease got in my hair, but I couldn't finish cleaning up until after my last class of the day. Of course Cronah said he didn't do it. He said he COULDN'T have done it, because Mrs. Pilton was giving him a test all morning. Yeah, right. Speaking of embarrassing, Cronah says something about Gaiana's braces every time he sees her. She joked that it's nice that we have one more thing in common — Cronah being mean to us. I'm trying to be as cool about it as she is.

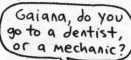

Gaiana, do you go to a dentist, or a mechanic?

JEDI LABYRINTH TRIAL

For the Jedi Labyrinth Trial, each student will begin from a different starting point. You will then find your way to the exit. Whenever you encounter another student, you are required to face off in a lightsaber fencing match. If you encounter more than one student at the same time, you may choose which student to duel. The loser of the match will have five minutes added to their finishing time.

You will be fitted with a tracking device that will keep score for matches, wins, losses, and encounters with other students. Losing three matches or taking more than one hour to complete the labyrinth will result in failing the semester. You are allowed only to bring your lightsaber with you. Be sure to eat a good breakfast, because no snacks will be allowed in the labyrinth due to the new carpet.

When your door opens, begin, your trial will!
Good luck, Roan!
You, too, Gaiana!
I wonder if there's anything else in here... probably only what we bring with us.
Here I go... my final test.

Oh, no!
Greer!
ZPTT!
BRZT!
BRZTKK!
BEEP!
Sorry, Greer!
Shrug
This looked a lot easier on paper...
Someone else must be this way...
ZAP!
VZZTK!
Gaiana!
ZZT!
BZT!
ZAPT!
BEEP!

Roan? Oh, no, do we have to fight now?!
AAAHHH!
Roan?!
SPRRKTT!
Aw, no fair! I was going to defeat her easy!
Too bad. We get to choose who we fight, and I choose you!
Go on, Gaiana! I need to handle this.
Good luck, Roan!
Fine. It'll be more fun to beat you!
Even if I do have some help...
Huh?
CLICK

Ronald? You can't team up on me!
Why not? We've been teaming up on you all year.
Huh?
It's been awesome. Filling your backpack with leftovers, greasing your door, cloning Voorpee... torturing you is fun!
Totally.
DARK SIDE HIGH FIVE!
RRRRRR.
Whoa, he's going to use his ANGER on us!
Ron? Ronald?
Where'd you go?
Looks like it's just you and me, Cronah!

BRRZZ
This is going to feel good, Roan.
BZT!
I'm going to cut you down to size!
Don't be so cocky, Cronah.
BRZAK!

TTKKT!!
OoF!
BRZT!
Ha!
Huh?!

ZRAPPTT!
BEEP!
NO!!
This isn't fair!
You got what you deserved, Cronah. Where are your friends now?
You don't have to gloat, Roan.
I'm not. I'm just glad you finally got payback for being such a jerk.
You're as much of a jerk as anyone. Where's your payback?

What are you talking about?
Ever since you got here, you've loved getting all the special attention. You have it easy. You've got a girlfriend and cool friends and good grades. You have it all.
I don't even have any good friends now. I'm not even going to become a Jedi probably, because of you.
Hey, Cronah...
What? Go ahead and rub it in some more.
When I got here, everyone else knew what they were doing. All I've tried to do is catch up, but I'm always screwing up.
Ha, that's true.
Even without you messing with me.
Maybe if you didn't mess with people, you'd have more friends.

Whatever. You're right, Roan. You're ALWAYS right.
No, I'm only right sometimes.
But I bet you'll still become a Jedi if you really want to.
I better get going...
I still need to find my way out of here.
Maybe this way?
I should turn right here...
Now left?
Dead end?! Ugh! I can't remember the map at all...
Wait, I don't need a MAP!
SMACK!
The Force will be my guide!

I know the way!
OOF!
I really need to remember to watch where I'm going when I use the Force.
Roan, you made it!
Did you finish first, Pasha?
No, Cyrus and I had an epic battle. We got here right after Gaiana.
First place, Gaiana? Good job!
Actually, I came in second. I couldn't have done it without you.
No, you did it on your own! Who came in first?
Hey, Roan! Good to see you finally made it.
Ronald was first?!
I'm finally at the top of the class!

He didn't REALLY come in first, because he CHEATED.
What are you talking about, buddy?
He has a map. Look.
Hmm, a serious accusation this is.
It's not true! Cronah put that there!
He also took a shortcut through an "Employees Only" door.
How do you know? I mean, no, I didn't!
HMPH. LET'S CHECK THE HOLORECORDER.
Holorecorder? No, that's not necessary!
HMPH.
That's not me!
Hmmm.

HEPTADAY

I knew Cronah had to be the one messing with me, and I knew Ronald is slimy, but I didn't realize they were working together to make me miserable. I actually feel kind of sorry for Cronah now. I know how he feels... thinking you're not any good, worrying about losing all of your friends. I'm just glad I didn't turn into a complete jerk like he was being. After the Labyrinth Trial, he at least seemed like he felt bad. A little. He told Master Yoda everything about Ronald cheating and all the pranks they played this year. Cronah acted like Ronald was the one who had all the ideas and was pushing him into doing stuff, but I don't know if I really believe that. Because he was honest (for once) and didn't use the map or employee shortcut, Cronah didn't get in as much trouble. He isn't graduating from Jedi Academy until he finishes a makeup summer school semester. Ronald, on the

He must've used Jedi mind tricks on me or something.
No way! Ronald? Mind tricks? Ha!

other hand, got in HUGE trouble, and they suspended him until further notice. He didn't seem too upset, like that was his plan the whole time.

Thank you, Master Yoda!

Principal Mar looked at Ronald's work from the past couple years and found he had been cheating a long time. I could have told them that. The cool thing is that, since Ronald cheated in the Labyrinth Trial, he was disqualified—so Gaiana finished first! She works so hard and never complains. She really deserved that. They gave her a cool medal for first place. We both agreed that it was a little too shiny. I finished in sixth place, which I feel pretty good about. Tomorrow, there's an end-of-the-year party. We'll all celebrate

I'm blinded!
Me, too!

~~graduateing~~ graduating from middle school. I can't believe that now when I say "It's over" it's not because I have to transfer to Plant School.

Too embarrassed to stick around for the graduation party, Ronald?

No, I've got orientation at the new school I'm transferring to.
What school is it, Cheater Academy?

Actually, it's my dream school: the Galactic Senate Academy! They were really impressed by my work here at Jedi Academy.
Hmph. Your work? Or everybody else's?

Ha, good one, Roan! You're right, though, I couldn't have done it without you. I'll make sure to thank you when I'm ruling the galaxy...
Please don't.

...and remember to vote for me!
Is he serious?
Uh, I think so.

The Padawan Observer End-of-the-Year Awards!
Best Student
Most Rhythmic
Best New Talent

Highest Flying

Best Friend

Greenest

Biggest Heart

Most Surprising

Most Mistaken for a Trash Can

Best Victory Dance

Least Likely to Laugh

Best Comic

Most in Need of a Haircut

Quietest

Best at Making Faces

Future Sith Lord

Toughest

Cuddliest
THE PADAWAN OBSERVER
VOL. MXIV #12

Bill, you're not going to D.J. the party?
All my equipment is packed up already. Plus, Master M'Ba-Tee really wanted to handle the music...
Not bad.
The food?
I haven't tried it yet...
I'm too nervous to.
It's cake, how bad can it be?
It is Gammy's cooking.
Here goes nothing.
GULP!
Oh, no, she's going to barf!
Lilly, talk to us!
It's...it's really good!
What?
The horrible taste has made her delusional.
No...it is good!
This is really good, Gammy!
HRURGG?
Er, like everything you cook!

Hi, Roan.
Gaiana! You look different...
I got my braces off!
No, it's not that...
Just kidding.
Stop!
Ha ha!
KISS!
Uh, I'll see you later, Roan.
Okay.
Hee hee.
BEEP BO BLOOP?
Heh heh heh!
Roan?
Are you okay?
Yep.
HMPH.

Jedi Academy

Jedi Academy Coruscant Campus

This certifies that

Roan Novachez

has completed the Padawan Course of study prescribed by the Jedi Council of the planet Coruscant and is therefore entitled to this

Diploma

In Testimony whereof, we have here unto affixed our signatures.

PRINCIPAL MAR

Principal

Master Yoda

Homeroom Instructor

MR. GARFIELD

Jedi Mentor

DUODAY (Best Duoday ever!)

I DID IT. It's official! I got my diploma. I actually completed Jedi Academy Middle School. I spent most of the past three years thinking I might fail, but when I look back now, I don't know why I worried so much. It wasn't always easy, but it was usually fun. I also thought I wouldn't make any friends, but I made the best friends ever. And Gaiana kissed me. ON THE LIPS. I can't even tell Dav about that, or it'll be next year before I hear the end of it. Plus, I'm a pilot! Sort of. I can't fly an actual starship by myself yet, but I passed all of my star-pilot training with Mr. G., so I can train in actual starships and not just simulators next year. Last year I would've been even more nervous about the future, but now even though I know there'll be lots of challenges and new things and I'll be

confused a lot of the time, I also know I can handle it. I'll miss Mr. Garfield, believe it or not. I think deep down inside he's a softie, and I'm sure he does like me. First of all, his comments on my report card were all positive this semester. There wasn't even a tiny "but" to any of it. Second, he gave me a graduation gift— a model of the ARC-170. And third, I thought

I got assigned to Mr. G. this year either because I wanted to be a pilot and that's one of his specialties, or it was just typical random fate. But I found out from Master Yoda that Mr. G. actually REQUESTED that I be assigned to him! And it wasn't because he wanted to torture me, but because he thought I had "real potential!" I wish I knew that BEFORE the school year!

Bye, Roan!
See you next year!
See you, guys!
Later, Roan.
See you next year, Cronah?
After I finish summer school. I won't have you there distracting me!
By the way, Cronah, some of those pranks...
Er...
You got some good ones on me.
Thanks, Roan.
And you better practice your lightsaber fencing...
I'm going to crush you in our rematch.
We'll see, Cronah.

Bye, Roan!
Bye, Lilly! Bye, Cyrus!
Roan, I'll miss Ewok Pilot. Have a good summer.
Thanks, Jo-Ahn.
That's like the second most she's ever talked to me.
Hey, Pasha! Hey, Shi-Fara!
Hey, Roan!
We're going to all get together this summer, right?
Definitely.
DOUBLE FIST BUMP WITH THE FORCE!
You two are funny. See ya, Roan!
Hi, Roan.
GAIANA!

So, um...
Ur, heh...
We'll see each other soon, right?
Of course!
SMECK!
Bye, Ro!
Pardon us, Master Roan, RW-22 would like to know if you need anything before you leave.
BEEP BO BLOOP!
No, I'm okay, thanks, T-P30.
BLIP BEEP!
You, too, RW-22.
pat pat
Hmph.
Oh, hi, Mr. Garfield.
I expect you to continue studying this summer.
Uh, sure. Heh!
What's funny?
Oh... well, it's just I used to think you might be a, um... Sith.

HA HA HA HA HA HA HA!
Phew!
You're funny, Roan. I like you.
Thanks, Mr. Garfield.
HMPH.
Hmmm. Right, I was, hm?
Well, you have done. A Jedi, you may yet become.
I guess so, Master Yoda.
Heh heh heh!
Of course, many more years of school, you have left. Heh heh!
Thanks for everything, Master Yoda!
May the Force be with you, hm?

Hi, Mom!
Hi, Ollie!
Roan! Roan!
Roan!
I'm be a Jedi!
I know, you want to be a Jedi.
No, I'm BE a Jedi!
See?
Jedi Kindergarten? That's great, Ollie!
Yayy!
But how did he get into—oh!
See? Look, Roan! See?
He couldn't wait to show you.
Congratulations, Roan!

Thanks, Dad! Look!
Your star pilot training license!
Hey, Dav.
Hey, Ro, so —
Wait! Did you?
Did I what?
You did! You and Gaiana!
Uh, no, what?
ON THE LIPS!
How did you know?
A brother knows.
What's Dav talking about, Roan?
Er, nothing.
So, Roan, should we take some practice flights? How about next week?
I wonder when school starts again?
Yeah!
Roan, what else aren't you telling me?
I want lightsaber!
THE END of middle school!

I don't know what happens next... but I can't wait!

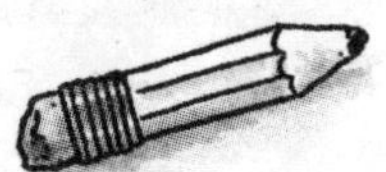

MAKE YOUR OWN COMIC BOOKS!

Think of a story that would be fun to draw!

Fold 3-4 sheets of paper in half and gather into a booklet.

Plan out what happens on each page with an outline!

Make the first page your cover. What will your comic book be about?

Drawing in pencil first will make it easy to change things and fix mistakes. When you're ready, trace over the pencil lines with an ink pen.

Unfold your pages. Have an adult help you make copies.

Put the copied pages back in order, fold, and staple!

Give out copies of your comic book to all your friends!

Jeffrey Brown is a cartoonist and author of the bestselling DARTH VADER AND SON and its sequels VADER'S LITTLE PRINCESS, GOODNIGHT DARTH VADER, and DARTH VADER AND FRIENDS as well as the STAR WARS: JEDI ACADEMY series. He lives in Chicago with his wife and two sons. Despite being a lifelong Star Wars fan, he still can't use the Force, but sometimes he likes to imagine that he can.

P.O. BOX 120 DEERFIELD IL 60015-0120 USA